BENEATH THE SHADOW OF
THE BLACK MOUNTAIN

Suddenly, Danilo stood up and left Wolfe and me sitting at the table.

In five minutes he was back with a wad of crumpled paper that he threw down next to his coffee cup. Wolfe asked him something in a polite tone.

Danilo picked up the paper, unfolded it, and showed us the contents.

It was a human finger.

Bantam Crime Line Books offer the finest in classic and modern American mysteries. Ask your bookseller for the books you have missed.

Rex Stout

The Black Mountain
Broken Vase
Death of a Dude
Death Times Three
Fer-de-Lance
The Final Deduction
Gambit
Plot It Yourself
The Rubber Band
Some Buried Caesar
Three for the Chair
Too Many Cooks

Max Allan Collins

The Dark City
Bullet Proof

A. E. Maxwell

Just Another Day in Paradise
Gatsby's Vineyard
The Frog and the Scorpion
Just Enough Light to Kill

Loren Estleman

Peeper

Dick Lupoff

The Comic Book Killer

Randy Russell

Hot Wire

V. S. Anderson

Blood Lies
King of the Roses

William Murray

When the Fat Man Sings
The King of the Nightcap

Eugene Izzi

King of the Hustlers
The Prime Roll
coming soon: Invasions

Gloria Dank

Friends Till the End
Going Out in Style

Jeffery Deaver

Manhattan Is My Beat
coming soon: Death of a Blue
Movie Star

Robert Goldsborough

Murder in E Minor
Death on Deadline
The Bloodied Ivy
The Last Coincidence

Sue Grafton

"A" Is for Alibi
"B" Is for Burglar
"C" Is for Corpse
"D" Is for Deadbeat
"E" Is for Evidence
"F" Is for Fugitive

David Lindsey

In the Lake of the Moon

Carolyn G. Hart

Design for Murder
Death on Demand
Something Wicked
Honeymoon with Murder
A Little Class on Murder

Annette Meyers

The Big Killing

Rob Kantner

Dirty Work
The Back-Door Man
Hell's Only Half Full

Robert Crais

The Monkey's Raincoat
Stalking the Angel

Keith Peterson

The Trapdoor
There Fell a Shadow
The Rain
Rough Justice

David Handler

The Man Who Died Laughing
The Man Who Lived by Night

Jerry Oster

Club Dead
Internal Affairs

A NERO WOLFE MYSTERY
THE BLACK MOUNTAIN
REX STOUT

BANTAM BOOKS
NEW YORK • TORONTO • LONDON • SYDNEY • AUCKLAND

THE BLACK MOUNTAIN

A Bantam Book / published by arrangement with
The Viking Press, Inc.

PRINTING HISTORY

Viking edition published October 1954
Dollar Mystery Guild edition published January 1955
Bantam edition / November 1955
11 printings through October 1989

ISBN 0-553-27291-8

Published simultaneously in the United States and Canada

Bantam Books are published by Bantam Books, a division of Bantam
Doubleday Dell Publishing Group, Inc. Its trademark, consisting of the
words "Bantam Books" and the portrayal of a rooster, is Registered in
U.S. Patent and Trademark Office and in other countries. Marca Regis-
trada. Bantam Books, 666 Fifth Avenue, New York, New York 10103.

PRINTED IN THE UNITED STATES OF AMERICA

KR   19   18   17   16   15   14   13   12   11

THE BLACK MOUNTAIN

WARNING

In a way this is a phony. A lot of the
talk I report was in languages I am not on
speaking terms with, so even with the
training I've had there is no use pretending
that here it is, word for word. But this
is what happened, and since I had to know
what was going on to earn my keep, Nero
Wolfe put it in English for me every chance
he got. For the times when it had to be on
the fly, and pretty sketchy, I have filled it in
as well as I could. Maybe I shouldn't
have tried to tell it at all,
but I hated to skip it.

ARCHIE GOODWIN

I

That was the one and only time Nero Wolfe had ever seen the inside of the morgue.

That Thursday evening in March I barely caught the phone call. With a ticket for a basketball game at the Garden in my pocket, I had dined in the kitchen, because I would have to leave the house at ten to eight, and Wolfe refuses to sit at table with one who has to pack it in and run. And that time I couldn't eat early because Fritz was braising a wild turkey and had to convey it to the dining room on a platter for Wolfe to see whole before wielding the knife. Sometimes when I have a date for a game or a show I get things from the refrigerator around six-thirty and take my time, but I wanted some of that hot turkey, not to mention Fritz's celery sauce and corn fritters.

I was six minutes behind schedule when, as I pushed my chair back and got erect, the phone rang. After asking Fritz to get it on the kitchen extension and proceeding to the hall, I had got my topcoat from the rack and was putting it on when Fritz called to me, "Archie! Sergeant Stebbins wants you!"

I muttered something appropriate for muttering but not for printing, made it to the office and across to my desk, lifted the receiver, and told it, "Shoot. You may have eight seconds."

It took more like eight times eighty, not because Purley Stebbins insisted on it, but I did after he had given me the main fact. When I had hung up I stood a while, frowning at Wolfe's desk. Many times through the years I have had the job of reporting something to Wolfe that I knew he wouldn't enjoy hearing, but this was different. This was tough. I even found myself wishing I had got away two minutes sooner, and then, realizing that that would have been tougher—for him, at least—I went to the hall, crossed it to the dining room, entered and spoke.

"That was Purley Stebbins. Half an hour ago a man came out of a house on East Fifty-fourth Street and was shot and killed by a man waiting there in a parked car. Papers found—"

1

Wolfe cut me off. "Must I remind you that business shall not intrude on meals?"

"You don't need to. This isn't business. Papers found on the body indicate that it was Marko Vukcic. Purley says there's no doubt about it, two of the dicks knew him by sight, but he wants me to come down and give positive identification. If you have no objection I'm going. It won't be as pleasant a way to spend an evening as going to a ball game, but I'm sure he would have done as much . . ."

I would have preferred to go on talking, but had to stop to clear my throat. Wolfe had put down his knife and fork, quietly and properly, on his plate. His eyes were leveled at me, but he wasn't scowling. A corner of his mouth twitched, and after a moment twitched again. To stop it he compressed his lips.

He nodded at me. "Go. Phone."

"Have you any—"

"No. Phone."

I whirled and went.

After going a block south on Tenth Avenue and flagging a taxi on Thirty-fourth Street, it didn't take long to roll cross-town to the city mortuary on East Twenty-ninth; and, since I was not a stranger there and was expected, I was passed through the railing and on in with no questions asked. I have never cared for the smell of that place. An assistant medical examiner named Faber tried once to sell me the idea that it smells just like a hospital, but I have a good nose and I didn't buy. He claimed that there are rarely more than one or two cadavers on the premises not in the coolers, and I said in that case someone must spray the joint with something to make it smell like a morgue.

The Homicide dick who escorted me down the corridor was one I knew only well enough to nod to, and the assistant ME in the room we entered was one I hadn't run across before. He was working on an object that was stretched out on a long table under a strong light, with a helper standing by. The dick and I stood and watched a minute. A detailed description of the performance would help only if you expect to be faced with the job of probing a corpse for a bullet that entered at an angle between the fifth and sixth ribs, so I won't go into it.

"Well?" the dick demanded.

"Yes," I told him. "I identify it as the body of Marko Vukcic, owner of Rusterman's Restaurant. If you want that signed, get it ready while I go use the phone."

2

I went out and down the corridor to the phone booth and dialed a number. Ordinarily when I am out of the house and phone in Fritz will answer after two or three signals or Wolfe will answer after five or six, but that time Wolfe's voice came before the first whirr was done.

"Yes?"

"Archie. It's Marko. Shot twice in the chest and once in the belly. I suppose Stebbins is up at Fifty-fourth Street, at the scene, and maybe Cramer too. Shall I go up there?"

"No. Stay where you are. I'm coming to look at him. Where is it?"

He had been making a living as a private detective in Manhattan for more than twenty years, and majoring in murder, and he didn't know where the morgue was. I told him; and, thinking that a little *esprit de corps* wouldn't be out of place in the circumstances, and knowing how he hated moving vehicles, I was going to suggest that I go get the sedan from the garage and drive him myself, but he hung up. I went out front to the sergeant at the desk, whose name was Donovan, and told him I had identified the body but Mr. Wolfe was coming to take a look and I would stick around.

Donovan shook his head. "I only got orders about you."

"Nuts. You don't need orders. Any citizen and taxpayer can enter here to look for the remains of a relative or friend or enemy. Mr. Wolfe is a citizen and taxpayer. I make out his tax returns."

"I thought you was a private eye."

"I don't like the way you say it, but I am. Also I am an accountant, an amanuensis, and a cocklebur. Eight to five you never heard the word amanuensis and you never saw a cocklebur."

He didn't rile. "Yeah, I know, you're an educated wit. For Nero Wolfe I need orders. I know too much about him. Maybe he can get away with his tricks with Homicide and the DA, but not with me or none of my guests."

I didn't feel like arguing. Besides, I knew Donovan had a lot to put up with. When the door opened to admit a customer it might be anything from a pair of hoodlums wanting to collect data for a fake identification, to a hysterical female wanting to find out if she was a widow. That must have got on his nerves. So I merely explained it to him. I told him a few things about Marko Vukcic. That he was one of the only ten men I knew of that Nero Wolfe called by their first names. That for years he had dined

3

once a month at Wolfe's table, and Wolfe and I had dined once a month at his restaurant. That he and Wolfe had been boys together in Montenegro, which was now a part of Yugoslavia. Donovan seemed to be listening, but he wasn't impressed. When I thought I had made the situation perfectly plain and stopped for breath, he turned to his phone, called Homicide, told them Wolfe was coming, and asked for instructions.

He hung up. "They'll call back," he informed me.

No bones got broken. His instructions came a minute before the door opened to admit Wolfe. I went and opened the gate in the railing, and Wolfe stepped through. "This way," I said and steered him to the corridor and along to the room.

The doctor had got the slug that had entered between the fifth and sixth ribs, and was going for the one lower down. I saw that from three paces off, where I stopped. Wolfe went on until the part of him that is farthest front, his middle, was touching the edge of the table. The doctor recognized him and spoke.

"I understand he was a friend of yours, Mr. Wolfe."

"He was," Wolfe said a little louder than necessary. He moved sidewise, reached a hand, put fingertips under Marko's chin, and pushed the jaw up so that the mouth closed; but when he took his hand away the lips parted again. He turned his head to frown at the doctor.

"That'll be arranged," the doctor assured him.

Wolfe nodded. He put fingers and a thumb into his vest pocket, withdrew them, and showed the doctor two small coins. "These are old dinars. I would like to fulfill a pledge made many years ago." The scientist said sure, go ahead, and Wolfe reached to Marko's face again, this time to place the coins on the eyes. The head was twisted a little, and he had to level it so the coins would stay put.

He turned away. "That's all. I have no further commitment to the clay. Come, Archie."

I followed him out and along the corridor to the front. The dick who had been my escort, there chinning with the sergeant, told me I didn't need to sign a statement and asked Wolfe if he verified the identification. Wolfe said he did and added, "Where's Mr. Cramer?"

"Sorry, I couldn't tell you."

Wolfe turned to me. "I told the driver to wait. You said East Fifty-fourth Street. Marko's address?"

"Right."

"We'll go there." He went, and I followed.

That taxi ride uptown broke a precedent. Wolfe's distrust of machinery is such that he is never in a condition to talk when he is being conveyed in something on wheels, even when I am driving, but that time he mastered it. He asked me questions about Marko Vukcic. I reminded him that he had known Marko a lot longer and better than I had, but he said there were some subjects which Marko had never discussed with him but might have with me—for example, his relations with women. I agreed that was logical, but said that as far as I knew Marko hadn't wasted time discussing his relations with women; he just went ahead and enjoyed them. I gave an instance. When, a couple of years previously, I had taken one named Sue Dondero to Rusterman's for dinner, Marko had cast an eye on her and contributed a bottle of one of his best clarets, and the next day had phoned to ask if I would care to give him her address and phone number, and I had done so and crossed her off. Wolfe asked why. I said to give her a break. Marko, sole owner of Rusterman's, was a wealthy man and a widower, and Sue might hook him. But she hadn't, Wolfe said. No, I agreed, as far as I knew there had been something wrong with the ignition.

"What the hell," the hackie grumbled, braking.

Having turned off Park Avenue into Fifty-fourth Street, he had made to cross Lexington, and a cop had waved him down. The cab stopped with a jerk that justified Wolfe's attitude toward machinery, and the hackie stuck his head out and objected.

"My fare's number is in that block, officer."

"Can't help it. Closed. Up or down."

He yanked the wheel, and we swung to the curb. I paid him, got out, and held the door, and Wolfe emerged. He stood a moment to take a deep breath, and we headed east. Ten paces along there was another cop, and a little farther on still another. Ahead, in the middle of the block, was a convention: police cars, spotlights, men working, and a gathering of citizens on the sidewalk across the street. On our side a stretch of the sidewalk was included in a roped-off area. As we approached it a cop got in the way and commanded, "Cross over and keep moving."

"I came here to look at this," Wolfe told him.

"I know. You and ten thousand more. Cross over."

"I am a friend of the man who was killed. My name is Nero Wolfe."

5

"Yeah, and mine's General MacArthur. Keep moving."

It might have developed into an interesting conversation if I hadn't caught sight, in one of the spotlights, of a familiar face and figure. I sang out, "Rowcliff!"

He turned and peered, stepped out of the glare and peered some more, and then approached. "Well?" he demanded.

Among all the array of Homicide personnel that Wolfe and I have had dealings with, high and low, Lieutenant Rowcliff is the only one of whom I am dead sure that our feelings are absolutely reciprocal. He would like to see me exactly where I would like to see him. So, having summoned him, I left it to Wolfe, who spoke.

"Good evening, Mr. Rowcliff. Is Mr. Cramer here?"

"No."

"Mr. Stebbins?"

"No."

"I want to see the spot where Mr. Vukcic died."

"You'll be in the way. We're working."

"So am I."

Rowcliff considered. He would have loved to order a couple of the help to take us to the river and dump us in, but the timing would have been bad. Since it was unheard of for Wolfe to leave his house to work as a matter of routine, he knew this was something extraordinary, and there was no telling how his superiors might react if he let his personal inclinations take charge. Of course he also knew that Wolfe and Vukcic had been close friends.

He hated to do it, but he said, "Come this way," and led us along to the front of the house and to the curb. "This is open to correction," he said, "but we think we've got it about right. Vukcic left the building alone. He passed between two parked cars to look west for a taxi. A car that was double-parked about twenty yards to the west—not a hack, a black or dark blue Ford sedan—started and came forward, and when it was about even with him an occupant of the car started shooting. It's not settled whether it was the driver or someone with him. We haven't found anyone that got a good look. He fell right there." Rowcliff pointed. "And stayed there. As you see, we're still at it here. Nothing from inside so far. Vukcic lived alone on the top floor, and there was no one there with him when he left. Of course he ate at his restaurant. Anything else?"

"No, thank you."

6

"Don't step off the curb. We're going over the pavement again in daylight." He left us.

Wolfe stood a moment, looking down at the spot on the pavement where Marko had dropped, then lifted his head to glance around. A moving spotlight hit his face and he blinked. Since that was the first time to my knowledge that he had ever started investigating a murder by a personal visit to the scene of the crime—not counting the occasions when he had been jerked loose by some other impulse, such as saving my life—I was curious to see how he would proceed. It was a chance he had seldom had.

He hopped on it by turning to me and asking, "Which way to the restaurant?"

I nodded west. "Up Lexington four blocks and around the corner. We can get a taxi—"

"No. We'll walk." He was off.

I went along, more and more impressed. The death of his oldest and closest friend had certainly hit him hard. He would have to cross five street intersections, with wheeled monsters waiting for him at every corner, ready to spring, but he strode on regardless, as if it were a perfectly natural and normal procedure.

II

Things were not natural and normal at Rusterman's. The six-foot, square-jawed doorman opened for us and let us pass through, and then blurted to Wolfe's broad back, "Is it true, Mr. Wolfe?" Wolfe ignored it and went on, but I turned and gave him a nod. Wolfe marched on past the cloakroom, so I did likewise. In the big front room, which you crossed on your way to the dining room, and which Marko had called the lounge but which I called the bar because it had one at its far side, there were only a few customers scattered around at the tables, since it was nearly nine-thirty and by that hour the clientele were inside, busy with *perdrix en casserole* or *tournedos Beauharnais*. The tone of the place, subdued but not stiff, had of course been set by Marko, with the able assistance of Felix, Leo, and Joe, and I had never seen one of them break training by so much as a flicker of an eyelash until that evening. As we entered, Leo, standing at the entrance to the dining room, caught sight of us and started toward us, then wheeled and went back and shouted into the dining room, "Joe!"

There were murmurs from the few scattered customers in the bar. Leo wheeled again, clapped his hand to his mouth, crossed to us, and stood staring at Wolfe. I saw sweat on his brow, another misdemeanor. In restaurants that sell squabs for five bucks or more apiece, captains and headwaiters are not allowed to sweat.

"It's true," Leo hissed, his hand still covering his mouth. He seemed to be shrinking in front of our eyes, and he was none too big anyway—not a shorty, but quite narrow up to his shoulders, where he spread out some. He let the hand fall, but kept his voice down. "Good God, Mr. Wolfe, is it true? It must—"

A hand gripped his shoulder from behind. Joe was there, and Joe was built for gripping. His years with Marko had polished him so that he no longer looked like a professional wrestler, but he had the size and lines.

"Get hold of yourself, damn it," he muttered at Leo. "Did you want a table, Mr. Wolfe? Marko's not here."

"I know he's not. He's dead. I don't—"

"Please not so loud. Please. Then you know he's dead?"

"Yes. I saw him. I don't want a table. Where's Felix?"

"Felix is up in the office with two men. They came and said Marko had been shot and killed. He left the dinner to Leo and me and took them upstairs. No one has been told except Vincent at the door because Felix said Marko would not want the dinner to be spoiled. It makes me want to vomit to see them eating and drinking and laughing, but it may be that Felix is right—and the face he had, it was no time to argue. Do you think he is right? I would myself want to put everybody out and lock the door."

Wolfe shook his head. "No. Felix is right. Let them eat. I'm going upstairs. Archie?" He headed for the elevator.

The third floor of the building had been remodeled a year or so previously to provide an office in front and three private dining rooms to the rear. Wolfe opened the door to the office, without knocking, and entered, and I followed. The three men in chairs over by a table turned to us. Felix Martin, a wiry, compact little guy with quick black eyes and gray hair—in his uniform, of course—got up and started toward us. The other two stayed put. They rated uniforms too, one an inspector's and the other a sergeant's, but didn't wear them to work.

"Mr. Wolfe," Felix said. You didn't expect a voice so deep from one that size, even after you were acquainted with it. "The worst thing on earth! The worst thing! Everything was going so fine!"

Wolf gave him a nod and went on by to Inspector Cramer. "What have you got?" he demanded.

Cramer controlled himself. His big round face was always a little redder, and his cold gray eyes a little colder, when he was exercising restraint. "I know," he conceded, "that you're interested in this one personally. Sergeant Stebbins was saying to me that we would have to make allowances, and I agreed. Also this is one time when I'll gladly take all the help you'll give, so let's all take it easy. Bring chairs, Goodwin."

For Wolfe I went and got the one at Marko's desk because it was nearer the size desired than any of the others. For myself I wasn't so particular. As I was joining the party Wolfe was demanding, not taking it easy at all, "Have you got anything?"

Cramer tolerated it. "Anything hot, no. The murder was committed just two hours ago."

"I know." Wolfe tried to shift to a more acceptable position in the chair. "Of course you have asked Felix if he can name the murderer." His eyes moved. "Can you, Felix?"

"No, sir. I can't believe it."

"You have no suggestions?"

"No, sir."

"Where have you been since seven o'clock?"

"Me?" The black eyes were steady at Wolfe. "I've been right here."

"All the time?"

"Yes, sir."

"Where has Joe been?"

"Right here too."

"All the time?"

"Yes, sir."

"You're sure of that?"

"Yes, sir."

"Where has Leo been?"

"Here too, all the time. Where else would we be at dinnertime? And when Marko didn't come—"

9

"If you don't mind," Cramer cut in, "I've already got this. I don't need—"

"I do," Wolfe told him. "I have a double responsibility, Mr. Cramer. If you assume that I intend to see that the murderer of my friend is caught and brought to account with the least possible delay, you are correct. But another onus is on me. Under my friend's will, as you will soon learn officially, I am executor of his estate and trustee ad interim. I am not a legatee. This restaurant is the only substantial asset, and it was left to six of the men who work here, with the biggest shares going to the three men I have just inquired about. They were told of the terms of the will when it was altered a year ago. Mr. Vukcic had no close relatives, and none at all in this country."

Cramer was eying Felix. "What's this place worth?"

Felix shrugged. "I don't know."

"Did you know that if Vukcic died you would be part owner of it?"

"Certainly. You heard what Mr. Wolfe said."

"You hadn't mentioned it."

"Good God!" Felix was out of his chair, on his feet, quivering. He stood a moment, got the quivering stopped, sat down again, and leaned forward at Cramer. "It takes time to mention things, officer. There is nothing about Marko and me, about him and us here, that I will not be glad to mention. He was hard about the work, hard and sometimes rough, and he could roar, but he was a great man. Listen, and I'll tell you how I feel about him. Here I am. Here at my side is Marko." Felix tapped his elbow with a finger. "A man appears and points a gun at him and is going to shoot. I jump to put myself in front of Marko. Because I am a big hero? No. I am no hero at all. Only because that's how I feel about Marko. Ask Mr. Wolfe."

Cramer grunted. "He was just asking you where you've been since seven o'clock. What about Leo and Joe? How do they feel about Marko?"

Felix straightened up. "They will tell you."

"How do you think they feel?"

"Not like me because they are not of my temperament. But to suppose it possible they would try to hurt him— never. Joe would not jump in front of Marko to stop the bullet. He would jump for the man with the gun. Leo—I don't know, but it is my opinion he would yell for help, for the police. I don't sneer at that; it would take more than a coward to yell for help."

10

"It's too bad one of you wasn't there when it happened," Cramer observed. It seemed to me uncalled-for. Obviously he didn't like Felix. "And you say you have no knowledge whatever of anyone who might have wanted Vukcic dead?"

"No, sir, I haven't." Felix hesitated. "Of course there is one thing—or I should say, more than one. There is women. Marko was a gallant man. Only one thing could ever take him away from his work here: a woman. I will not say that to him a woman was more important than a sauce —he could not be accused of ever neglecting a sauce—but he had a warm eye for women. After all, it was not essential for him to be in the kitchen when everything was planned and ready, and Joe and Leo and I are competent for the tables and service, so if Marko chose to enjoy dinner at his own table with a guest there was no feeling about it among us. But it might have caused feeling among others. I have no personal knowledge. Myself, I am married with four children and have no time, but everybody knows that women can arouse strong feelings."

"So he was a chaser," Sergeant Stebbins growled.

"Pfui!" Wolfe growled back at him. "Gallantry is not always a lackey for lust."

Which was a fine sentiment with company present, but the fact remained that Wolfe had himself asked me about Marko's relations with women. For the next three hours, there in Marko's office, that subject came close to monopolizing the conversation. Felix was dismissed and told to send Joe up. Other Homicide dicks arrived, and an assistant district attorney, and waiters and cooks were brought up for sessions in the private dining rooms; and with each one, after a few personal questions, the emphasis was on the female guests who had eaten at Marko's own table in the past year or so. By the time Wolfe was willing to call it a day and got himself erect and stretched, it was well after midnight and a respectable bulk of data had been collected, including the names of seven women, none of them notorious.

Cramer rasped at Wolfe, "You said you intend to see that the murderer is caught and brought to account with the least possible delay. I don't want to butt in, but I'll just mention that the Police Department will be glad to help."

Wolfe ignored the sarcasm, thanked him politely, and headed for the door.

On the way downtown in the cab I remarked that I had

11

been pleased to note that no one had pronounced the name of Sue Dondero. Wolfe, on the edge of the seat, gripping the strap, set to jump for his life, made no reply.

"Though I must say," I added, "there were enough of them without her. They're not going to like it much. By noon tomorrow there'll be thirty-five dicks, five to a candidate, working on that list. I mention it merely for your consideration, in case you are thinking of telling me to have all seven of them in the office at eleven in the morning."

"Shut up," he muttered.

Usually I react to that command vocally, but that time I thought it just as well to obey. When we rolled to the curb in front of the old brownstone on West Thirty-fifth Street I paid the driver, got out and held the door for Wolfe, mounted the seven steps to the stoop, and opened the door with my key. After Wolfe had crossed the threshold I closed the door and put the chain bolt on, and when I turned Fritz was there and was telling Wolfe, "There's a lady to see you, sir."

It popped into my mind that it would save me a lot of trouble if they were going to drop in without being invited, but Fritz was adding, "It's your daughter, Mrs. Britton."

There was a faint suggestion of reproach in Fritz's tone. For years he had disapproved of Wolfe's attitude toward his adopted daughter. A dark-haired Balkan girl with an accent, she had appeared out of the blue one day long ago and proceeded to get Wolfe involved in an operation that had been no help to the bank account. When it was all over she had announced that she didn't intend to return to her native land, but neither did she intend to take any advantage of the fact that she had in her possession a paper, dated in Zagreb years before, establishing her as the adopted daughter of Nero Wolfe. She had made good on both intentions, having got a job with a Fifth Avenue travel agency, and having, within a year, married its owner, one William R. Britton. No friction had developed between Mr. and Mrs. Britton and Mr. Wolfe, because for friction you must have contact, and there had been none. Twice a year, on her birthday and on New Year's Day, Wolfe sent her a bushel of orchids from his choicest plants, but that was all, except that he had gone to the funeral when Britton died of a heart attack in 1950.

That was what Fritz disapproved of. He thought any man, even Nero Wolfe, should invite his daughter, even an adopted one, to dinner once in a while. When he expressed that opinion to me, as he did occasionally, I told him that he knew damn well that Carla found Wolfe as irritating as he found her, so what was the use?

I followed Wolfe into the office. Carla was in the red leather chair. As we entered she got up to face us and said indignantly, "I've been waiting here over two hours!"

Wolfe went and took her hand and bowed over it. "At least you had a comfortable chair," he said courteously, and went to the one behind his desk, the only one in the world he thoroughly approved of, and sat. Carla offered me a hand with her mind elsewhere, and I took it without bowing.

"Fritz didn't know where you were," she told Wolfe.

"No," he agreed.

"But he said you knew about Marko."

"Yes."

"I heard it on the radio. I was going to go to the restaurant to see Leo, then I thought I would go to the police, and then I decided to come here. I suppose you were surprised, but I wasn't."

She sounded bitter. She looked bitter too, but I had to admit it didn't make her any less attractive. With her dark eyes flashing, she might still have been the young Balkan damsel who had bounded in on me years before.

Wolfe's eyes had narrowed at her. "If you are saying that you came here and waited two hours for me on account of Marko's death, I must ask why. Were you attached to him?"

"Yes."

Wolfe shut his eyes.

"If I know," she said, "what that word means—attached. If you mean attached as a woman to a man, no, of course not. Not like that."

Wolfe opened his eyes. "Then how?"

"We were attached in our devotion to a great and noble cause! The freedom of our people! And your people! And there you sit making faces! Marko has told me—he has asked you to help us with your brains and your money, and you refused!"

"He didn't tell me you were in it. He didn't mention you."

"I suppose not." She was scornful. "He knew that would make you sneer even more. Here you are, rich and fat and happy with your fine home and fine food and your glass rooms on the roof with ten thousand orchids for you to

13

smirk at, and with this Archie Goodwin for a slave to do all the work and take all the danger! What do you care if the people of the land you came from are groaning under the heel of the oppressor, with the light of their liberty smothered and the fruits of their labor snatched from them and their children at the point of the sword? *Stop making faces!*"

Wolfe leaned back and sighed deeply. "Apparently," he said dryly, "I must give you a lecture. I grimaced neither at your impudence nor at your sentiment, but at your diction and style. I condemn clichés, especially those that have been corrupted by fascists and communists. Such phrases as 'great and noble cause' and 'fruits of their labor' have been given an ineradicable stink by Hitler and Stalin and all their vermin brood. Besides, in this century of the overwhelming triumph of science, the appeal of the cause of human freedom is no longer that it is great and noble; it is more or less than that; it is essential. It is no greater or nobler than the cause of edible food or the cause of effective shelter. Man must have freedom or he will cease to exist as man. The despot, whether fascist or communist, is no longer restricted to such puny tools as the heel or the sword or even the machine gun; science has provided weapons that can give him the planet; and only men who are willing to die for freedom have any chance of living for it."

"Like you?" She was disdainful. "No. Like Marko. He died."

Wolfe flapped a hand. "I'll get to Marko. As for me, no one has ordained you as my monitor. I make my contributions to the cause of freedom—they are mostly financial—through those channels and agencies that seem to me most efficient. I shall not submit a list of them for your inspection and judgment. I refused to contribute to Marko's project because I distrusted it. Marko was himself headstrong, gullible, oversanguine, and naïve. He had—"

"For shame! He's dead, and you insult—"

"That will do!" he roared. It stopped her. He went down a few decibels. "You share the common fallacy, but I don't. I do not insult Marko. I pay him the tribute of speaking of him and feeling about him precisely as I did when he lived; the insult would be to smear his corpse with the honey excreted by my fear of death. He had no understanding of the forces he was trying to direct from a great distance, no control of them, and no effective check on their honor or

14

fidelity. For all he knew, some of them may be agents of Tito, or even of Moscow—"

"That isn't true! He knew all about them—anyway, the leaders. He wasn't an idiot, and neither am I. We do check on them, all the time, and I—Where are you going?"

Wolfe had shoved his chair back and was on his feet. "You may not be an idiot," he told her, "but I am. I was letting this become a pointless brawl when I should have known better. I'm hungry. I was in the middle of dinner when the news came of Marko's death. It took my appetite. I tried to finish anyway, but I couldn't swallow. With an empty stomach, I'm a dunce, and I'm going to the kitchen and eat something." He glanced up at the wall clock. "It's nearly two o'clock. Will you join me?"

She shook her head. "I had dinner. I couldn't eat."

"Archie?"

I said I could use a glass of milk and followed him out. In the kitchen Fritz greeted us by putting down his magazine, leaving his chair, telling Wolfe, "Starving the live will not profit the dead," and going to open the refrigerator door.

"The turkey," Wolfe said, "and the cheese and pineapple. I've never heard that before. Montaigne?"

"No, sir." Fritz put the turkey on the table, uncovered it, and got the slicer and handed it to Wolfe. "I made it up. I knew you would have to send for me, or come, and I wished to have an appropriate remark ready for you."

"I congratulate you." Wolfe was wielding the knife. "To be taken for Montaigne is a peak few men can reach."

I had only had milk in mind, but Fritz's personal version of cottage cheese with fresh pineapple soaked in white wine is something that even a Vishinsky wouldn't veto. Also Wolfe offered me a wing and a drumstick, and it would have been unsociable to refuse. Fritz fixed a tasty tray and took it in to Carla, but when Wolfe and I rejoined her, some twenty minutes later, it was still untouched on the table at her elbow. I admit it could have been that she was too upset to eat, but I suspected her. She knew damn well that it irritated Wolfe to see good food turned down.

Back at his desk, he frowned at her. "Let's see if we can avoid contention. You said earlier that you supposed I was surprised, but that you weren't. Surprised at what?"

She was returning the frown. "I don't—oh, of course. Surprised that Marko was murdered."

"And you weren't?"

"No."

"Why not?"

"Because of what he was doing. Do you know what he was doing?"

"Circumstantially, no. Tell me."

"Well, in the past three years he has put nearly sixty thousand dollars of his own money into the cause, and he has collected more than half a million. He has gone seven times to Italy to confer with leaders of the movement who crossed the Adriatic to meet him. He has sent twelve men and two women over from this country to help—three Montenegrins, three Slovenians, two Croats, and six Serbs. He has had things printed and arranged for them to get to the peasants. He has sent over many tons of supplies, many different things—"

"Weapons? Guns?"

She gave it a thought. "I don't know. Of course, that would be against the law—American law. Marko had a high regard for American law."

Wolfe nodded. "Not unmerited. I didn't know he was in so deep. So you are assuming that he was murdered because of these activities. That either Belgrade or Moscow regarded him as a menace, or at least an intolerable nuisance, and arranged for his removal. Is that it?"

"Yes."

"Belgrade or Moscow?"

Carla hesitated. "I don't know. Of course there are those who secretly work with the Russians all over Yugoslavia, but more in Montenegro than other parts, because it is next to Albania, and Albania is ruled by the puppets of the Russians."

"So are Hungary and Rumania and Bulgaria."

"Yes, but you know the border between Montenegro and Albania. You know those mountains."

"I do indeed. Or I did." From the look on Wolfe's face, the emotions aroused by the memory were mixed. "I was nine years old the first time I climbed the Black Mountain." He shrugged it off. "Whether Belgrade or Moscow, you think they had an agent in New York, or sent one, to deal with Marko. Do you?"

"Of course!"

"Not of course if it is merely a surmise. Can you validate it? Have you any facts?"

"I have the fact that they hated him and he was a danger to them."

16

Wolfe shook his head. "Not that kind. Something specific—a name, an act, a thing said."

"No."

"Very well. I accept your surmise as worthy of inquiry. How many persons are there in and around New York, other than contributors of money, who have been associated with Marko in this?"

"Why, altogether, about two hundred."

"I mean closely associated. In his confidence."

She had to think. "Four or five. Six, counting me."

"Give me their names and addresses and phone numbers. Archie, take them down."

I got my notebook and pen and was ready, but nothing came. I looked at her. She was sitting with her dark Montenegrin eyes focused on Wolfe, her chin up and her lips pressed together.

"Well?" he demanded.

"I don't trust you," she said.

Naturally he would have liked to tell me to bounce her, and I must say I couldn't have blamed him, but she wasn't just a prospective client with a checkbook. She had or might have something he needed for paying a personal debt. So he merely barked at her. "Then why the devil did you come here?"

They glared at each other. It was not a sight to impel me to hurry up and get married and have a daughter, especially not an adopted one.

She broke the tableau. "I came because I had to do something. I knew if I went to the police they would want me to tell everything about us, and I couldn't do that because some of the things some of us do—well, you asked about sending weapons." She fluttered a hand. "But Marko was your good friend, and he thought you were his, and you have a famous reputation for catching murderers, and after all I still have that paper that says I am your daughter, so I came without really thinking. Now I don't know. You refused to give money to the cause. When I speak of freedom and the oppressor you make a face. It is true you have Montenegrin blood, you are of the race that fought back the savage Turks for five hundred years, but so are others, still in those mountains, who are licking the bloody feet of the tyrant. Have I looked into your heart? How do I know who you serve? How do I know if you too get your orders from Belgrade or Moscow?"

"You don't," Wolfe said bluntly.

She stared at him.

"You are not a fool," he assured her. "On the contrary, you would be a fool if you took my probity for granted, as little as you know of me. As far as you know it's quite possible that I'm a blackguard. But you haven't thought it through. To test your surmise about the death of Marko I need some facts from you, but what are they? Names and addresses and dates—things that are already known to the enemy. I have no means of convincing you that I am not verminous, so I offer a suggestion. I will ask you questions. You will assume that I am a Communist, owing allegiance either to Belgrade or Moscow, no matter which. You will also assume—my vanity insists on it—that I am not far from the top in the councils of depravity. So. Each question I put, ask yourself if it isn't extremely likely either that I already know the answer or that it is readily available to me. If yes, tell me. If no, don't. The way I act on the information will show you whether you should trust me, but that's unimportant."

She was concentrating on it. "It's a trick."

He nodded. "And rather ingenious. For the record, I say that your misgiving about me is groundless; but assuming that I am of the enemy, I'll certainly try to pry something out of you that I don't already have, so you must keep your wit sharp. Shall we start and see how it goes?"

She didn't like it "You might tell the police. We are not criminals, but we have a right to our secrets, and the police could make it very difficult."

"Bosh. You can't have everything. You can't have me both a Communist agent and a police informer; I'm not a chameleon. You're making it a travesty, and you might as well go. I'll manage without you."

She studied him. "All right. Ask me."

"Eat something first. That food is still palatable."

"No, thank you."

"Beer, then? A glass of wine? Whisky?"

"No, thank you. Nothing."

"I'm thirsty. Archie? Beer, please. Two bottles."

I went to the kitchen for it.

III

Three weeks and eight hours later, at eleven in the morning of the second Friday in April, Wolfe descended from the plant rooms in his elevator, entered the office, crossed to the chair at his desk, and sat.

As usual, I had opened the morning mail, gone through it, and put it on his blotter under a paperweight. "That memo on top needs immediate attention," I told him. "Cartright of Consolidated Products is being gypped again, or thinks he is. Last time he paid our bill for twelve grand without a squeak. You're to call him."

He shoved the paperweight off with such enthusiasm that it rolled across the desk and off to the floor. Then he picked up the pile of mail, squeezed it into a ball between his hands, and dropped it into his wastebasket.

Of course it was childish, since he knew darned well I would retrieve it later, but it was a nice gesture, and I fully appreciated it. The humor he was in, it wouldn't have surprised me any if he had taken the other paperweight, a hunk of carved ebony that had once been used by a man named Mortimer to crack his wife's skull, and fired it at me. And the humor I was in, I probably wouldn't have bothered to dodge.

There had been plenty of activity during those 512 hours. Saul Panzer, Fred Durkin, and Orrie Cather had all been summoned the first morning and given errands, and had been paid a total of $3,143.87, including expenses. I had put in a good sixteen hours a day, part in the office and part on the go. Wolfe had worked on thirty-one different people, mostly at his desk, but for five of them who couldn't be wrangled in he had gone outdoors and traveled, something he had never done for a fee. Among the hours he had spent on the phone had been time for six calls to London, five to Paris, and three to Bari in Italy.

Of course all that had been only a dab compared to the capers of the cops. As the days went by and lead after lead petered out, things would have simmered down if it hadn't been for the papers. They kept hot on it for two reasons: first, they had a suspicion there were international compli-

19

cations and wanted to smoke them out; and second, they thought it was the joke of the year that Nero Wolfe's best friend had been croaked, and Wolfe was supposed to be working on it, but apparently no one had even been nominated for a charge, let alone elected. So the papers kept it going, and the law couldn't relax a little even if it wanted to. Cramer had called on Wolfe five times, and Stebbins more than that, and Wolfe had been downtown twice to conferences at the DA's office.

We had dined nine times at Rusterman's, and Wolfe had insisted on paying the check, which probably broke another precedent—for an executor of an estate. Wolfe went early to spend an hour in the kitchen, and twice he raised hell— once about a Mornay sauce and once about a dish which the menu called *Suprêmes de Volaille en Papillote*. I would have suspected he was merely being peevish if the look on the chefs' faces hadn't indicated that he was absolutely right.

Of course Cramer and his army had covered all the routine. The car the shots had been fired from had been hot, stolen an hour earlier from where it had been parked on West Fifty-sixth Street, and abandoned soon after the shooting, on Second Avenue. The scientists, from finger-print-lifters and bullet-gazers on up, had supplied a lot of dope but no answers, and the same goes for the three or four dozen who went after the woman angle, which after a couple of weeks was spread to include several more, going back four years instead of one, in addition to the original seven. One day Cramer told Wolfe he could go over the whole file if he wanted to, some three hundred reports of sessions with eighty-four people, and Wolfe took him up. He spent eleven hours at it, at the DA's office. The only result was that he made nine suggestions, all of which were followed, and none of which opened a crack.

He left the women and the feelings they had aroused to the cops, and kept Saul and Fred and Orrie, not to mention me, on the international angle. A great deal was accomplished. We learned a lot about the ten organizations listed in the Manhattan phone directory whose names began with "Yugoslav." Also that Serbs don't care much for Bosnians, and less for Croats. Also that the overwhelming majority of the Yugoslavs in New York are anti-Tito, and practically all of them are anti-Russian. Also that eight per cent of the doormen on Park Avenue are Yugoslavs. Also that New Yorkers who are, or whose parents were, from Yugoslavia are fairly cagey about opening up to strangers and are inclined to shut the valves tight if they get the notion that you're being nosy. Also many other things, including a few that seemed to offer a faint hope of starting a trail that could lead to the bird who had put three bullets in Marko Vukcic; but they all blew a fuse.

In the first four days of the three weeks we saw Carla twice more. Saturday noon she came and asked Wolfe if it was true, as announced, that there would be no funeral. He said yes, in accordance with Marko's wish, in writing, that he be cremated and that there should be no services. She objected that there were hundreds of people who wanted to show their respect and love for him, and Wolfe replied that if a man's prejudices were to be humored at all after he was no longer around to impose them, surely he should be allowed to dictate the disposal of his own clay. The best she could get was a promise that the ashes would be delivered to her. Then she had asked about progress in the investigation, and he had said he would report when there was anything worth reporting, which hadn't satisfied her at all.

She came again late Monday afternoon. I had had enough of answering the damn doorbell and left it to Fritz. She came charging in and across to Wolfe's desk, and blurted at him, "You told the police! They've had Leo down there all day, and this afternoon they went to Paul's place and took him too! I knew I shouldn't trust you!"

"Please—" Wolfe tried, but she had pulled the cork and it had to come. He leaned back and shut his eyes. She went on ranting until she had to stop for breath. He opened his eyes and inquired, "Are you through?"

"Yes! I'm *all* through! With you!"

"Then there's no more to say." He jerked his head. "There's the door."

She went to the red leather chair and sat on the edge. "You said you wouldn't tell the police about us!"

"I did not." He was disgusted and tired. "Since you mistrust me you will credit nothing I say, so why should I waste words?"

"I want to hear them!"

"Very well. I have said nothing to the police about you or your associates or your surmise about Marko's death, but they are not donkeys, and I knew they would get onto it. I'm surprised it took them so long. Have they come to you?"

21

"No."

"They will, and it's just as well. I have only four men, and we are getting nowhere. They have regiments. If you tell them about coming to see me Thursday night they'll resent my withholding it, but that's of no consequence. Tell them or not, as you please. As for giving them the information you gave me, do as you please about that too. It might be better to let them dig it up for themselves, since in the process they might uncover something you don't know about. So much for that. Since you're here I may as well tell you what progress I have made. None." He raised his voice. "None!"

"Nothing at all?"

"Nothing."

"I won't tell the police what I told you, but that doesn't matter. If you haven't, you will." Suddenly she was on her feet with her arms spread out. "Oh, I need you! I need to ask you—I need to tell you what I must do! But I won't! I won't!" She turned and was gone. She moved so fast that when I got to the hall she already had the front door open. By the time I reached it she was out and the door was shut. Through the one-way glass panel I saw her going down the steps, sure and supple, like a fencer or a dancer, which was reasonable, since she had been both.

That was the last we saw of her during the three weeks, but not the last we heard. Word of her came four days later, Friday morning, from an unexpected quarter. Wolfe and I were having a session in the office with Saul and Fred and Orrie, one of a series, trying to think up some more stones to look under, when the doorbell rang and a moment later Fritz entered to announce, "A man to see you, sir. Mr. Stahl of the Federal Bureau of Investigation."

Wolfe's brows went up; he glanced at me, I shook my head, and he told Fritz to bring the man in. The hired help, including me, exchanged glances. An FBI man was no rare spectacle for any of us, but Stahl wasn't just one of the swarm; he had worked up to where he gave more orders than he took, and the word was that by Christmas he would be occupying the big corner room down at 290 Broadway. He didn't often go out to run errands, so it was quite an event for him to drop in, and we all knew it and appreciated it. When he entered and marched across to Wolfe's desk and offered a hand, Wolfe even did him the honor of rising to shake, which showed how desperate the situation was.

"It's been quite a while since I saw you last," Stahl observed. "Three years?"

Wolfe nodded. "I believe so." He indicated the red leather chair, which Fred Durkin had vacated. "Be seated."

"Thank you. May we make this private?"

"If necessary." Wolfe glanced at the trio, and they got up and filed out and shut the door. Stahl went and sat. Medium-sized and beginning to be a little short on hair, he wasn't impressive to look at, except his jaw, which came straight down a good two inches and then jutted forward. He was well designed for ramming. He gave me a look, and Wolfe said, "As you know, Mr. Goodwin is privy to all that I hear and see and do."

Stahl knew no such thing, because it wasn't true. I'd like to have a nickel—or make it a dime, with the dollar where it is—for every item Wolfe has withheld from me just for the hell of it.

Stahl merely nodded. "In a way," he said, "you might consider this a personal matter—personal to you. We want to get in touch with your daughter, Mrs. Carla Britton."

Wolfe's shoulders went up an eighth of an inch and down again. "Then do so. Her address is nine-eighty-four Park Avenue. Her phone number is Poplar three-three-oh-four-three."

"I know. She hasn't been there since Tuesday, three days ago. She left no word with anyone. Nobody knows where she is. Do you?"

"No, sir."

Stahl passed a fingertip across the prow of his chin. "One thing I like about you, you prefer things put plain and straight. I've never seen the room upstairs, right above yours, that you call the South Room, but I've heard about it. You've been known to use it for guests, clients and otherwise, from time to time. Do you mind if I go up and take a look at it?"

Wolfe shrugged again. "It will be wasted energy, Mr. Stahl."

"That's all right, I have some to spare."

"Then go ahead. Archie?"

"Yes, sir." I went and opened the door to the hall and, with Stahl at my heels, went to the stairs and mounted the two flights. At the door to the South Room I stepped aside and told him politely, "You go first. She might shoot." He opened the door and went in, and I crossed the sill. "It's nice and sunny," I said, "and the beds are first-rate." I

23

pointed. "That door's the bathroom, and that's a closet. A girl named Priscilla Eads once rented it for fifty bucks a day, but she's dead. I'm pretty sure Mr. Wolfe would shade that for a prominent public servant like you. . . ."

I saved it because he was moving. He knew he had drawn a blank, but he went and opened the door to the bathroom and looked in, and on his way back detoured to open the door to the closet for a glance. As he retreated to the hall I told his back, "Sorry you don't like it. Would you care to take a look at my room just down the hall? Or the plant rooms, just one flight up?" I kept trying to sell him on the way downstairs. "You might like Mr. Wolfe's own room better—the bed has a black silk coverlet. I'll be glad to show it to you. Or if you want a bargain there's a couch in the front room."

He entered the office, returned to his chair, focused on Wolfe, and inquired, "Where is she?"

Wolfe focused back. "I don't know."

"When did you see her last?"

Wolfe straightened in his chair. "Aren't you being crass, sir? If this inquisition isn't gratuitous, warrant it."

"I told you she has been away from her home for three days and we can't find her."

"That doesn't justify your tramping in here and branding me a liar."

"I didn't."

"Certainly you did. When I said I didn't know where she was you proceeded to search my house for her. When you didn't find her you demanded to know where she is. Pfui."

Stahl smiled like a diplomat. "Well, Goodwin evened it up by riding me. I guess I'd better start over. You know we are aware of your qualities and abilities. We know you don't need to have a thing all spelled out for you. I didn't think I'd have to tell you that my coming here and asking about Mrs. Britton meant that we are interested in some aspects of the investigation into the murder of Marko Vukcic, that we have reason to think he was engaged in activities that are the proper concern of the federal government, that your daughter was associated with him in those activities, and that her disappearance is therefore a matter for inquiry. I might as well add that as yet we have no evidence that you have been connected with those activities in any way, either loyally with Vukcic or subversively."

Wolfe snorted. "I have not applied for a certificate of virtue."

"No. You wouldn't. I might also add that I have discussed this with Inspector Cramer and he knows I'm here. We learned of Mrs. Britton's involvement only last night. To put it all on the table, her disappearance suggests two possibilities: one, that she has been dealt with as Vukcic was, by the same person or persons; and two, that she was double-crossing Vukcic, working for the Communists, and was in on the plan to kill him and helped with it, and it was getting too hot for her here. Is that enough to warrant the question, when did you see her last?"

"The answer won't help you much. In this room four days ago, Monday afternoon, about six-thirty. She was here not more than ten minutes. She gave no hint of an intention to disappear or of any reason for such an intention. Of your two possibilities, I advise you to dismiss the second, but that will not necessarily leave only the first; there are others."

"Why dismiss the second?"

Wolfe cocked his head. "Mr. Stahl. The miasma of distrust that has poisoned the air we breathe is so pervasive that it reduced you to the fatuity of going up to look in my South Room. I would have liked then to tell you to leave, but I couldn't afford the gesture because I'm up a stump. I've been hunting the murderer of Marko Vukcic for eight days now, and am floundering in a bog, and if there is any chance that you can offer a straw I want it. So I'll tell you all I know about Mrs. Britton's connection with this affair."

He did so in full, making no objection to Stahl's getting out his notebook and taking notes. At the end he observed, "You asked why I advised you to dismiss the second of your two possibilities, and that's my answer. You will discount it as your caution may dictate. Now I would appreciate a straw. With your prerogatives and resources, you must have one to toss me."

I had never heard or seen him being abject before, and in spite of the strain he was under I didn't care for it. Stahl didn't either. He smiled, and I would have liked to wipe it off with one hand. He glanced at his wristwatch and rose from the chair. He didn't even bother to say he was late for an appointment. "This is something new," he stated. "Nero Wolfe asking for a straw. We'll think it over. If you hear from your daughter, or of her, we'll appreciate it if you'll let us know."

When I returned to the office after letting him out I told Wolfe, "There are times when I wish I hadn't been taught manners. It would have been a pleasure to kick his ass down the stoop."

"Get them in here," he growled. "We must find her."

But we didn't. We certainly tried. It is true that Stahl and Cramer had it on us in prerogatives and resources, but Fred Durkin knows how to dig, Orrie Cather is no slouch, Saul Panzer is the best operative north of the equator, and I have a good sense of smell. For the next six days we concentrated on picking up a trace of her, but we might as well have stayed up in my room and played pinochle. Not a glimmer. It was during that period that Wolfe made most of his long-distance calls to London and Paris and Bari. At the time I thought he was just expanding the bog to flounder in, and I still think he was merely making some wild stabs, but I have to admit it was Hitchcock in London and Bodin in Paris who finally put him onto Telesio in Bari; and if he hadn't found Telesio we might still be looking for Carla and for the murderer of Marko. I also admit that I regard myself as the one for hunches around this joint, and I resent anyone horning in, even Wolfe. His part is supposed to be brainwork. However, what matters is that if he hadn't got in touch with Telesio and talked with him forty bucks' worth, in Italian, the Tuesday after Stahl's visit, he would never have got the calls from Telesio.

There were three of them. The first one came Thursday afternoon while I was out tracking down a lead that Fred thought might get somewhere. When I got back to the office just before dinner Wolfe snapped at me, "Get them here this evening for new instructions."

"Yes, sir." I went to my desk, sat, and swiveled to face him. "Any for me?"

"We'll see." He was glowering. "I suppose you have to know. I had a call from Bari. It is now past midnight in Italy. Mrs. Britton arrived in Bari at noon and left a few hours later in a small boat to cross the Adriatic."

I goggled. "How the hell did she get to Italy?"

"I don't know. My informant may, but he thinks it necessary to use discretion on the phone. I am taking it that she's there. For the present we shall keep it to ourselves. The new instructions for Saul and Fred and Orrie will be on the ground that it is more urgent to disclose the murderer than to find Mrs. Britton. As for—"

"Saul will smell it. He'll know."

26

"Let him. He won't know where she is, and even if he did, no matter. Who is more trustworthy, Saul or you?"

"I would say Saul. I have to watch myself pretty close."

"Yes. As for Mr. Cramer and Mr. Stahl, we owe them nothing. If they're still looking for her they may find someone else." He sighed way down, leaned back, and shut his eyes, presumably to try to devise a program for the hired help.

So the first call from Telesio didn't stop operations, it merely changed the strategy. With the second one it was different. It came four days later, at two-thirty a.m. Monday. Of course it was half-past eight in the morning at Bari, but I was in no shape to manage that calculation as I yanked myself enough awake to realize that I hadn't dreamed it—the phone was ringing. I rolled over and reached for it. When I heard that it was a call from Bari, Italy, for Mr. Nero Wolfe I told the operator to hold it, turned on the light, went and flipped the switch controlling the gong that splits the air if anyone steps within ten feet of the door of Wolfe's room at night, and then descended one flight and knocked. His voice came, and I opened the door and entered and pushed the wall switch.

He made a magnificent mound under the electric blanket, lying there blinking at me. "Well?" he demanded.

"Phone call from Italy. Collect."

He refuses to concede the possibility that he will ever be willing to talk on the phone while in bed, so the only instrument in his room is on a table over by a window. I went and switched it on. He pushed the blanket back, maneuvered his bulk around and up, made it over to the table in his bare feet, and took the phone. Even in those circumstances I was impressed by the expanse of his yellow pajamas.

I stood and listened to a lingo that I didn't have in stock, but not for long. He didn't even get his money's worth, for it had been less than three minutes when he cradled the thing, gave me a dirty look, padded back to the bed, lowered himself onto its edge, and pronounced some word that I wouldn't know how to spell.

He went on. "That was Signor Telesio. His discretion has been aggravated into obscurity. He said he had news for me, that was clear enough, but he insisted on coding it. His words, translated: 'The man you seek is within sight of the mountain.' He would not elucidate, and it would have been imprudent to press him."

27

I said, "I've never known you to seek a man harder or longer than the guy who killed Marko. Does he know that?"

"Yes."

"Then the only question is, which mountain?"

"It may safely be presumed that it is Lovchen—the Black Mountain, from which Montenegro got its name."

"Is this Telesio reliable?"

"Yes."

"Then there's no problem. The guy that killed Marko is in Montenegro."

"Thank you." He twisted around, got his legs onto the bed and under the blanket, and flattened out, if that term may be used about an object with such a contour. Folding the end of the yellow sheet over the edge of the blanket, he pulled it up to his chin, turned on his side, said, "Put the light out," and closed his eyes.

He was probably asleep before I got back upstairs.

That leaves four days of the three weeks to account for, and they were by far the worst of the whole stretch. It was nothing new that Wolfe was pigheaded, but that time he left all previous records way behind. He knew damn well the subject had got beyond his reach and he was absolutely licked, and the only intelligent thing to do was to hand it over to Cramer and Stahl, with a fair chance that it would get to the CIA, and, if they happened to have a tourist taking in the scenery in those parts, they might think it worth the trouble to give him an errand. Not only that, there were at least two VIPs in Washington, one of them in the State Department, whose ears were accessible to Wolfe on request.

But no. Not for that mule. When—on Wednesday evening, I think it was—I submitted suggestions as outlined above, he rejected them and gave three reasons. One, Cramer and Stahl would think he had invented it unless he named his informant in Bari, and he couldn't do that. Two, they would merely nab Mrs. Britton if and when she returned to New York, and charge her with something and make it stick. Three, neither the New York police nor the FBI could reach to Yugoslavia, and the CIA wouldn't be interested unless it tied in with their own plans and projects, and that was extremely unlikely.

Meanwhile—and this was really pathetic—he kept Saul and Fred and Orrie on the payroll and went through the motions of giving them instructions and reading their re-

28

ports, and I had to go through with my end of the charade. I don't think Fred and Orrie suspected they were just stringing beads, but Saul did, and Wolfe knew it. Thursday morning Wolfe told me it wouldn't be necessary for Saul to report direct to him, that I could take it and relay it.

"No, sir," I said firmly. "I'll quit first. I'll play my own part in the goddam farce if you insist on it, but I'm not going to try to convince Saul Panzer that I'm a halfwit. He knows better."

I have no idea how long it might have gone on. Sooner or later Wolfe would have had to snap out of it, and I prefer to believe it would have been sooner. There were signs that he was beginning to give under the strain—for instance, the scene in the office the next morning, Friday, which I have described. As for me, I was no longer trying to needle him. I was merely offering him a chance to shake loose when I told him the memo from Cartright of Consolidated Products needed immediate attention and reminded him that Cartright had once paid a bill for twelve grand without a squeak, and it looked hopeful when he shoved the paperweight off the desk and dumped the mail in the wastebasket. I was deciding how to follow through and keep him going when the phone rang, and I would have liked to treat it as Wolfe had treated the mail. I turned and got it. A female voice asked me if I would accept a collect call from Bari, Italy, for Mr. Nero Wolfe, and I said yes and told Wolfe. He lifted his instrument.

It was even briefer than it had been Sunday night. I am not equipped to divide Italian into words, but my guess was that Wolfe didn't use more than fifty altogether. From his tone I suspected it was some more unwelcome news, and his expression as he hung up verified it. He tightened his lips, glaring at the phone, and then transferred the glare to me.

"She's dead," he said glumly.

It always irritated him if I talked like that. He had drilled it into me that when giving information I must be specific, especially in identifying objects or persons. But since the call had been from Bari, and there was only one female in that part of the world that we were interested in, I didn't raise the point.

"Where?" I asked. "Bari?"

"No. Montenegro. Word came across."

"What or who killed her?"

"He says he doesn't know, except that she died violently.

29

He wouldn't say she was murdered, but certainly she was. Can you doubt it?"

"I can, but I don't. What else?"

"Nothing. But for the bare fact, nothing. Even if I could have got more out of him, what good would it do me, sitting here?"

He looked down at his thighs, then at the right arm of his chair, then at the left arm, as if to verify the fact that he really was sitting. Abruptly he shoved his chair back, arose, and moved. He went to the television cabinet and stood a while staring at the screen, then turned and crossed to the most conspicuous object in the office, not counting him— the thirty-six-inch globe—twirled it, stopped it, and studied geography a minute or two. He about-faced, went to his desk, picked up a book he was halfway through—*But We Were Born Free* by Elmer Davis—crossed to the bookshelves, and eased the book in between two others. He turned to face me and inquired, "What's the bank balance?"

"A little over twenty-six thousand, after drawing the weekly checks. You put the checks in the wastebasket."

"What's in the safe?"

"A hundred and ninety-four dollars and twelve cents in petty, and thirty-eight hundred in emergency reserve."

"How long does it take a train to get to Washington?"

"Three hours and thirty-five minutes to four hours and fifteen minutes, depending on the train."

He made a face. "How long does it take an airplane?"

"Sixty to a hundred minutes, depending on the wind."

"How often does a plane go?"

"Every thirty minutes—on the hour and the half."

He shot a glance at the wall clock. "Can we make the one that leaves at noon?"

I cocked my head. "Did you say *'we'*?"

"Yes. The only way to get passports in a hurry is to go after them in person."

"Where do we want passports for?"

"England and Italy."

"When are we leaving?"

"As soon as we get the passports. Tonight if possible. Can we make the noon plane for Washington?"

I stood up. "Look," I said, "it's quite a shock to see a statue turn into a dynamo without warning. Is this just an act?"

"No."

30

"You've told me over and over not to be impetuous. Why don't you sit down and count up to a thousand?"

"I am not being impetuous. We should have gone days ago, when we learned he was there. Now it is imperative. Confound it, can we make that plane?"

"No. Nothing doing. God knows what you'll be eating for the next week—or maybe year—and Fritz is working on shad roe mousse Pocahontas for lunch, and if you miss it you'll take it out on me. While I phone the airline and get your naturalization certificate and my birth certificate from the safe, you might go and give Fritz a hand since you're all of a sudden in such a hell of a hurry."

He was going to say something, decided to skip it, and turned and headed for the kitchen.

IV

We got back home at nine o'clock that evening, and we had not only the passports but also seats on a plane that would leave Idlewild for London at five the next afternoon, Saturday.

Wolfe was not taking it like a man. I had expected him to quit being eccentric about vehicles, since he had decided to cross an ocean and a good part of a continent, and relax, but there was no visible change in his reactions. In the taxis he sat on the front half of the seat and gripped the strap, and in the planes he kept his muscles tight. Apparently it was so deep in him that the only hope would be for him to get analyzed, and there wasn't time for that. Analyzing him would take more like twenty years than twenty hours.

Washington had been simple. The VIP in the State Department, after keeping us waiting only ten minutes, had tried at first to explain that high-level interference with the Passport Division was against policy, but Wolfe interrupted him, not as diplomatically as he might have under that roof. Wolfe asserted that he wasn't asking for interference, merely for speed; that he had come to Washington instead of handling it through New York because a professional emergency required his presence in London at the earliest possible moment; and that he had assumed the

VIP's professions of gratitude for certain services rendered, and expressions of willingness to reciprocate, could reasonably be expected to bear the strain of a request so moderate and innocent. That did it, but the technicalities took a while anyway.

Saturday was crowded with chores. There was no telling how long we would be away. We might be back in a few days, but Wolfe had to have things arranged for an indefinite absence, so I had my hands full. Fred and Orrie were paid off. Saul was signed up to hold down the office and sleep in the South Room. Nathaniel Parker, the lawyer, was given authority to sign checks, and Fritz was empowered to take charge at Rusterman's. Theodore was given bales of instructions that he didn't need about the orchids. The assistant manager of the Churchill Hotel obliged by cashing a check for ten grand, in tens and twenties and Cs, and I spent a good hour getting them satisfactorily stashed in a belt I bought at Abercrombie's. The only squabble the whole day came at the last minute, as Wolfe stood in the office with his hat and coat on, and I opened a drawer of my desk and got out the Marley .32 and two boxes of cartridges.

"You're not taking that," he stated.

"Sure I am." I slipped the gun into my shoulder holster and dropped the boxes into a pocket. "The registration for it is in my wallet."

"No. It may make trouble at the customs. You can buy one at Bari before we go across. Take it off."

It was a command, and he was boss. "Okay," I said, and took the gun out and returned it to the drawer. Then I sat down in my chair. "I'm not going. As you know, I made a rule years ago never to leave on an errand connected with a murder case without a gun, and this is a super errand. I'm not going to try chasing a killer around a black mountain in a foreign land with nothing but some damn popgun I know nothing about."

"Nonsense." He looked up at the clock. "It's time to go."

"Go ahead."

Silence. I crossed my legs. He surrendered. "Very well. If I hadn't let you grow into a habit I could have done this without you. Come on."

I retrieved the Marley and put it where it belonged, and we departed. Fritz and Theodore escorted us to the sidewalk and the curb, where Saul sat at the wheel of the sedan.

The luggage was in the trunk, leaving all the back seat for Wolfe. From the woebegone look on Fritz's and Theodore's faces we might have been off for the wars, and in fact they didn't know. Only Saul and Parker had been shown the program.

At Idlewild we got through the formalities and into our seats on the plane without a hitch. Thinking it wouldn't hurt Wolfe to have a little comic relief to take his mind off the perils of the takeoff, I told him of an amusing remark I had overheard from someone behind us as we had ascended the gangway. "My God," a voice had said, "they soak me thirty dollars for overweight baggage, and look at him." Seeing it didn't produce the desired effect, I fastened my seat belt and left him to his misery.

I admit he didn't make a show of it. For the first couple of hours I hardly saw his face as he sat staring through the window at the ocean horizon or the clouds. We voted to have our meal on trays, and when it came, fricassee and salad with trimmings, he did all right with it, and no snide remarks or even looks. Afterward I brought him two bottles of beer and was properly thanked, which was darned plucky of him, considering that he held that all moving parts of all machinery are subject to unpredictable whim, and if the wrong whim had seized our propellers we would have dropped smack into the middle of the big drink in the dead of night.

On that thought I went to sleep, sound. When I woke up my watch said half-past two, but it was broad daylight and I smelled fried bacon, and Wolfe's voice was muttering at my ear, "I'm hungry. We're ahead of time, and we'll be there in an hour."

"Did you sleep?"

"Some. I want breakfast."

He ate four eggs, ten slices of bacon, three rolls, and three cups of coffee.

I still haven't seen London, because the airport is not in London and Geoffrey Hitchcock was there at the gate waiting for us. We hadn't seen him since he had last been in New York, three years before, and he greeted us cordially for an Englishman and took us to a corner table in a restaurant, and ordered muffins and marmalade and tea. I was going to pass, but then I thought what the hell, I might as well start here as anywhere getting used to strange foreign food, and accepted my share.

Hitchcock took an envelope from his pocket. "Here are

33

your tickets for the Rome plane. It leaves in forty minutes, at twenty after nine, and arrives at three o'clock, Rome time. Since your luggage is being transferred directly to it, the custom chaps here don't want you. We have half an hour. Will that be enough?"

"Ample." Wolfe dabbed marmalade on a muffin. "Mostly I want to know about Telesio. Thirty years ago, as a boy, I could trust him with my life. Can I now?"

"I don't know."

"I need to know," Wolfe snapped.

"Of course you do." Hitchcock used his napkin on his thin, pale lips. "But nowadays a man you can trust farther than you can see is a rare bird. I can only say I've been dealing with him for eight years and am satisfied, and Bodin has known him much longer, from back in the Mussolini days, and he vouches for him. If you have—"

A cracking metallic voice, probably female, from a loudspeaker split the air. It sounded urgent. When it stopped I asked Hitchcock what she had said, and he replied that she was announcing that the nine-o'clock plane for Cairo was ready at Gate Seven.

"Yeah." I nodded. "I thought I heard Cairo. What language was she talking?"

"English."

"I *beg* your pardon," I said politely and sipped some tea.

"I was saying," he went on to Wolfe, "that if you have to trust someone on that coast I doubt if you could do better than Telesio. From me that's rather strong, for I'm a wary man."

Wolfe grunted. "It's better than I hoped for. One other thing—a plane at Rome for Bari."

"Yes." Hitchcock cleared his throat. "One has been chartered and should be in readiness." He took a worn old leather case from his pocket, fingered in it, and extracted a slip of paper. "You should be met on arrival, but if there's a hitch here's the name and phone number." He handed it over. "Eighty dollars, and you may pay in dollars. The agent I deal with in Rome, Giuseppe Drogo, is a good man by Roman standards, but he is quite capable of seeking some trivial personal advantage from his contact with his famous American fellow. Of course he had to have your name. If it is now all over Rome, I must disclaim responsibility."

Wolfe did not look pleased, which showed how concentrated he was on his mission. Any man only one-tenth as conceited as he was couldn't help but glow at being told that his name was worth scattering all over Rome. As for Hitchcock, the British might be getting short on empire, but apparently they still had their share of applesauce.

A little later the loudspeaker announced in what I guess was English that the plane for Rome was ready, and our host convoyed us out to the gate and stood by to watch us take the air. As we taxied to the runway Wolfe actually waved to him from the window.

With Wolfe next to the window, I had to stretch my neck for my first look at Europe, but it was a nice sunny day and I kept a map open on my knee, and it was very interesting, after crossing the Strait of Dover, to look toward Brussels on the left and Paris on the right, and Zurich on the left and Geneva on the right, and Milan on the left and Genoa on the right. I recognized the Alps without any trouble, and I actually saw Bern. Unfortunately I missed looking toward Florence. Passing over the Apennines a little to the north, we hit an air pocket and dropped a mile or so before we caught again, which is never much fun, and some of the passengers made noises. Wolfe didn't. He merely shut his eyes and set his jaw. When we had leveled off I thought it only civil to remark, "That wasn't so bad, That time I flew to the Coast, going over the Rockies we—"

"Shut up," he growled.

So I missed looking toward Florence. We touched concrete at the Rome airport right on the nose, at three o'clock of a fine warm Sunday afternoon, and the minute we descended the gangway and started to walk across to the architecture my association with Wolfe, and his with me, changed for the worse. All my life, needing a steer in new surroundings, all I had had to do was look at signs and, if that failed, ask a native. Now I was sunk. The signs were not my kind. I stopped and looked at Wolfe.

"This way," he informed me. "The customs."

The basic setup between him and me was upset, and I didn't like it. I stood beside him at a table and listened to the noises he exchanged with a blond basso, my only contribution being to produce my passport when told to do so in English. I stood beside him at a counter in another room and listened to similar noises, exchanged this time with a black-haired tenor, though I concede that there I played a more important part, being permitted to open the bags and close them again after they had been inspected. More

35

noises to a redcap with a mustache who took over the bags —only his cap was blue. Still more, out in the sunshine, with a chunky signor in a green suit with a red carnation in his lapel. Wolfe kindly let me in on that enough to tell me that his name was Drogo and that the chartered plane for Bari was waiting for us. I was about to express my appreciation for being noticed when a distinguished-looking college boy, dressed for a wedding or a funeral, stepped up and said in plain American, "Mr. Nero Wolfe?"

Wolfe glared at him. "May I ask your name, sir?"

He smiled amiably. "I'm Richard Courtney from the embassy. We thought you might require something, and we would be glad to be of service. Can we help you in any way?"

"No, thank you."

"Will you be in Rome long?"

"I don't know. Must you know?"

"No, no." He perished the thought. "We don't want to intrude on your affairs—just let us know if you need any information, any assistance at all."

"I shall, Mr. Courtney."

"Please do. And I hope you won't mind—" From the inside breast pocket of his dark gray tailored coat that had not come from stock he produced a little black book and a pen. "I would like very much to have your autograph." He opened the book and proffered it. "If you will?"

Wolfe took the book and pen, wrote, and handed them back. The well-dressed college boy thanked him, urged him not to fail to call on them for any needed service, included Drogo and me in a well-bred smile, and left us.

"Checking on you?" I asked Wolfe.

"I doubt it. What for?" He said something to Drogo and then to the bluecap, and we started off, with Drogo in the lead and the bluecap with the bags in the rear. After a stretch on concrete and a longer one on gravel of a color I had never seen, we came to a hangar, in front of which a small blue plane was parked. After the one we had crossed Europe in it looked like a toy. Wolfe stood and scowled at it a while and then turned to Drogo and resumed the noises. They got louder and hotter, then simmered down a little, and finally ended by Wolfe telling me to give him ninety dollars.

"Hitchcock said eighty," I objected.

"He demanded a hundred and ten. As for paying in advance, I don't blame him. When we leave that contraption we may be in no condition to pay. Give him ninety dollars."

I shelled it out, was instructed to give the bluecap a buck and did so after he had handed the luggage up to the pilot, and steadied the portable stile while Wolfe engineered himself up and in. Then I embarked. There was space for four passengers, but not for four Wolfes. He took one seat and I the other, and the pilot stepped on it, and we rolled toward the runway. I would have preferred not to wave to Drogo on account of the extra sawbuck he had chiseled, but for the sake of public relations I flapped a mitt at him.

Flying low over the Volscian hills—see map—in a pint-sized plane was not an ideal situation for a chat with my fellow passenger, but it was only ninety minutes to Bari, and something had to get settled without delay. So I leaned across and yelled to him above the racket, "I want to raise a point!"

His face came around to me. It was grim. I got closer to his ear. "About the babble. How many languages do you speak?"

He had to jerk his mind onto it. "Eight."

"I speak one. Also I understand one. This is going to be too much for me. What I see ahead will be absolutely impossible except on one condition. When you're talking with people, I can't expect you to translate as you go along, but you will afterward, the first chance we get. I'll try to be reasonable about it, but when I ask for it I want it. Otherwise I might as well ride this thing back to Rome."

His teeth were clenched. "This is a choice spot for an ultimatum."

"Nuts. You might as well have brought a dummy. I said I'll be reasonable, but I've been reporting to you for a good many years and it won't hurt you to report to me for a change."

"Very well. I submit."

"I want to be kept posted in full."

"I said I submit."

"Then we can start now. What did Drogo say about the arrangements for meeting Telesio?"

"Nothing. Drogo was told only that I wanted a plane for Bari."

"Is Telesio meeting us at the airport?"

"No. He doesn't know we're coming. I wanted to ask Mr. Hitchcock about him first. In nineteen twenty-one he killed two Fascisti who had me cornered."

"What with?"

"A knife."

"In Bari?"

"Yes."

"I thought you were Montenegrin. What were you doing in Italy?"

"In those days I was mobile. I have submitted to your ultimatum, as you framed it, but I'm not going to give you an account of my youthful gestes—certainly not here and now."

"What's the program for Bari?"

"I don't know. There was no airport then, and I don't know where it is. We'll see." He turned away to look through the window. In a moment he turned back. "I think we're over Benevento. Ask the pilot."

"I can't, damn it! I can't ask anybody anything. You ask him."

He ignored the suggestion. "It must be Benevento. Glance at it. The Romans finished the Samnites there in three hundred and twelve B.C."

He was showing off, and I approved. Only two days earlier I would have given ten to one that up in an airplane he wouldn't have been able to remember the date of anything whatever, and here he was rattling off one twenty-two centuries back. I went back to my window for a look down at Benevento. Before long I saw water ahead and to the left, my introduction to the Adriatic, and watched it spread and glisten in the sun as we sailed toward it; and then there was Bari floating toward us. Part of it was a jumble on a neck stretched into the sea, apparently with no streets, and the other part, south of the neck along the shore, had streets as straight and regular as midtown Manhattan, with no Broadway slicing through.

The plane nosed down.

V

From here on, please have in mind the warning I put at the front of this. As I said, I have had to do some filling in, but everything important is reported as Wolfe gave it to me.

Sure, it was five o'clock of a fine April Sunday afternoon,

Palm Sunday, and our plane was unscheduled, and Bari is no metropolis, but even so you might have expected to see some sign of activity around the airport. None. It was dead. Of course there was someone in the control tower, and also presumably someone in the small building which the pilot entered, presumably to report, but that was all except for three boys throwing things at a cat. From them Wolfe learned where a phone was and entered a building to use it. I stood guard over the bags and watched the communist boys. I assumed they were communists because they were throwing things at a cat on Palm Sunday. Then I remembered where I was, so they could have been fascists.

Wolfe came back and reported. "I reached Telesio. He says the guard on duty at the front of this building knows him and should not see him get us. I phoned a number he gave me and arranged for a car to come and take us to a rendezvous."

"Yes, sir. It'll take me a while to get used to this. Maybe a year will do it. Let's get in out of the sun."

The wooden bench in the waiting room was not too comfortable, but that wasn't why Wolfe left it after a few minutes and went outside to the front. With three airplanes and four thousand miles behind him, he was simply full of get-up-and-go. It was incredible, but there it was: I was inside sitting down, and he was outside standing up. I considered the possibility that the scene of his youthful gestes had suddenly brought on his second childhood, and decided no. He was suffering too much. When he finally reappeared and beckoned to me, I lifted the bags and went.

The car was a shiny long black Lancia, and the driver wore a neat gray uniform trimmed in green. There was plenty of room for the bags and us too. As we started off, Wolfe reached for the strap and got a good hold on it, so he was still fundamentally normal. We swung out of the airport plaza onto a smooth black-top road, and without a murmur the Lancia stretched its neck and sailed, with the speedometer showing eighty, ninety, and on up over a hundred—when I realized it was kilometers, not miles. Even so, it was no jalopy. Before long there were more houses, and the road became a street, then a winding avenue. We left it, turning right, got into some traffic, made two more turns, and pulled up at the curb in front of what looked like a railroad station. After speaking with the driver Wolfe told me, "He says four thousand lire. Give him eight dollars."

I audited it mentally as I got my wallet, certified it, and handed it over. The tip was apparently acceptable, since he held the door for Wolfe and helped me get the bags out. Then he got in and rolled off. I wanted to ask Wolfe if it was a railroad station, but there was a limit. His eyes were following something, and, taking direction, I saw that he was watching the Lancia on its way. When it turned a corner and disappeared he spoke.

"We have to walk five hundred yards."

I picked up the bag. *"Andiamo."*

"Where the devil did you get that?"

"Lily Rowan, at the opera. The chorus can't get off the stage without singing it."

We set out abreast, but soon the sidewalk was just wide enough for me and the bags, so I let him lead. I don't know whether one of his youthful gestes had been to pace off that particular route, which included three straightaways and three turns, but if so his memory was faulty. It was more like half a mile, and if it had been much farther the bags would have begun to get heavy. A little beyond the third turn, in a street narrower than any of the others, a car was parked, with a man standing alongside. As we approached he stared rudely at Wolfe. Wolfe stopped practically against him and said, "Paolo."

"No." The man couldn't believe it. "Yes, by God, it is. Get in." He opened the car door.

It was a little two-door Fiat that would have done for a tender for the Lancia, but we made it—me with the bags in the back, and Wolfe with Telesio in front. As the car went along the narrow street, with Telesio jerking his head sidewise every second to look at Wolfe, I took him in. I had seen dozens of him around New York—coarse, thick hair, mostly gray; dark, tough skin; quick black eyes; a wide mouth that had done a lot of laughing. He began firing questions, but Wolfe wasn't talking, and I couldn't blame him. I was willing to keep my mind open on whether Telesio was to be trusted as a brother, but in less than a mile it was already closed about trusting him as a chauffeur. Apparently he had some secret assurance that all obstructions ahead, animate or inanimate, would disappear before he got there, and when one didn't and he was about to make contact, his split-second reaction was very gay. When we got to our destination and I was out of it on my feet, I circled the Fiat for a look at the fenders. Not a sign of a scratch, let alone a dent. I thought to myself, a man in a million, thank God.

The destination was a sort of courtyard back of a small white two-story stuccoed house, with flowers and a little pool and high walls on three sides. "Not mine," Telesio said. "A friend of mine who is away. At my place in the old city you would be seen by too many people before I know your plans."

Actually it was two hours later that I learned he had said that, but I'm going to put things in approximately where people said them. That's the only way I can keep it straight.

Telesio insisted on carrying the bags in, though he had to put them down to use a key on the door. In a small square hall he took our hats and coats and hung them up, and ushered us through into a good-sized living room. It was mostly pink, and one glance at the furniture and accessories settled it as to the sex of his friend—at least I hoped so. Wolfe looked around, saw no chair that even approached his specifications, crossed to a couch, and sat. Telesio disappeared and came back in a couple of minutes with a tray holding a bottle of wine, glasses, and a bowl of almonds. He filled the glasses nearly to the brim, gave us ours, and raised his.

"To Ivo and Garibaldi!" he cried.

We drank. They left some, so I did. Wolfe raised his glass again. "There is only one response. To Garibaldi and Ivo!"

We emptied the glasses. I found a comfortable chair. For an hour they talked and drank and ate almonds. When Wolfe reported to me later he said that the first hour had been reminiscent, personal and irrelevant, and their tone and manner certainly indicated it. A second bottle of wine was needed, and another bowl of almonds. What brought them down to business was Telesio's raising his glass proposing, "To your little daughter Carla! A woman as brave as she was beautiful!"

They drank. By then I was merely a spectator. Wolfe put his glass down and spoke in a new tone. "Tell me about her. You saw her dead?"

Telesio shook his head. "No, I saw her alive. She came to me one day and wanted to go across. I knew about her from Marko, on his trips to meet them from over there, and of course she knew all about me. I tried to tell her it was no job for a woman, but she wouldn't listen. She said that with Marko dead she must see them and arrange what to do. So I brought Guido to her, and she paid him too much to take her across, and she went that day. I tried—"

"Do you know how she got here from New York?"

"Yes, she told me—as a stewardess on a ship to Naples, which was mere routine with certain connections, and from Naples by car. I tried to phone you before she got away, but there were difficulties, and by the time I got you she had gone with Guido. That was all I could tell you. Guido returned four days later. He came to my place early in the morning, and with him was one of them—Josip Pasic. Do you know of him?"

"No."

"Anyway he is too young for you to remember. He brought a message from Danilo Vukcic, who is a nephew of Marko. The message was that I was to phone to you and say these words: 'The man you seek is within sight of the mountain.' I knew you would want more and I tried to get more, but that was all Josip would say. He hasn't known me for many years as the older ones have. So that was all I could tell you. Naturally I thought it meant that the man who had killed Marko was there, and was known. Did you?"

"Yes."

"Then why didn't you come?"

"I wanted something better than a cryptogram."

"Not as I remember you—but then, you are older, and so am I. You are also much heavier and have more to move, but that is no surprise, since Marko told me about you and even brought me a picture of you. Anyway, now you are here, but your daughter is dead. I can't believe how you got here. It was only Friday, forty-eight hours ago, that I phoned you. Josip came again, not with Guido this time, in another boat, with another message from Danilo. I was to inform you that your daughter had died a violent death within sight of the mountain. Again that was all he would say. If I had known you were coming I would have tried to keep him here for you, but he has gone back. In any case, you will want to see Danilo himself, and for him we will have to send Guido. Danilo will trust only Guido. He could be here—let's see—Tuesday night. Early Wednesday morning. You can await him here. Marko used this place. I believe, in fact, he paid for this wine, and he

42

wouldn't want us to spare it, and the bottle is empty. That won't do."

He left the room and soon was back with another bottle, uncorked. After filling Wolfe's glass he came to me. I would have preferred to pass, but his lifted brows at my prior refusal had indicated that a man who went easy on wine would bear watching, so I took it and got another handful of almonds.

"This place isn't bad," he told Wolfe, "even for you who live in luxury. Marko liked to do his own cooking, but I can get a woman in tomorrow."

"It won't be necessary," Wolfe said. "I'm going over."

Telesio stared. "No. You must not."

"On the contrary. I must. Where do we find this Guido?"

Telesio sat down. "You mean this?"

"Yes. I'm going."

"In what form and what capacity?"

"My own. To find the man who killed Marko. I can't enter Yugoslavia legally, but among those rocks and ravines what's the difference?"

"That's not the problem. The worst Belgrade would do to Nero Wolfe would be to ship him out, but the rocks and ravines are not Belgrade. Nor are they what you remember. Precisely there, around that mountain, are the lairs of the Tito cutthroats and the Albanian thugs from across the border who are the tools of Russia. They reached to kill Marko in far-off America. They killed your daughter within hours after she stepped ashore. She may have exposed herself by carelessness, but what you propose—to appear among them as yourself—would be greatly worse. If you are so eager to commit suicide, I will favor you by providing a knife or a gun, as you may prefer, and there will be no need for you to undertake the journey across our beautiful sea, which is often rough, as you know. I would like to ask a question. Am I a coward?"

"No. You were not."

"I am not. I am a very brave man. Sometimes I am astonished at the extent of my courage. But nothing could persuade me, known as I am, to show myself between Cetinje and Scutari day or night—much less to the east, where the border crosses the mountains. Was Marko a coward?"

"No."

"That is correct. But he never even considered risking

himself in that hive of traitors." Telesio shrugged. "That's all I have to say. Unfortunately you will not be alive for me to say I told you so." He picked up his glass and drained it.

Wolfe looked at me to see how I was taking it, realized that I would have nothing to take until he got a chance to report, and heaved a deep sigh. "That's all very well," he told Telesio, "but I can't hunt a murderer from across the Adriatic with the kind of communications available, and now that I've got this far I am not going to turn around and go home. I'll have to consider it and discuss it with Mr. Goodwin. In any event, I'll need this Guido. What's his name?"

"Guido Battista."

"He is the best?"

"Yes. That is not to say he is a saint. The list of saints to be found today in this neighborhood would leave room here." He passed a fingertip over the nail of his little finger.

"Can you bring him here?"

"Yes, but it may take hours. This is Palm Sunday." Telesio stood up. "If you are hungry, the kitchen is equipped and there are some items in the cupboard. There is wine but no beer. Marko told me of your addiction to beer, which I deplore. If the phone rings you may lift it, and if it is me I will speak. If I do not speak you should not. No one is expected here. Draw the curtains properly before you turn lights on. Your presence in Bari may not be known, but they reached to Marko in New York. My friend would not like blood on this pretty pink rug." Suddenly he laughed. He roared with laughter. "Especially not in such a quantity! I will find Guido."

He was gone. The sound came of the outer door closing, and then of the Fiat's engine as it turned in the courtyard and headed for the street.

I looked at Wolfe. "This is fascinating," I said bitterly.

He didn't hear me. His eyes were closed. He couldn't lean back comfortably on the couch, so as a makeshift he was hunched forward.

"I know you're chewing on something," I told him, "but I'm along and I have nothing to chew on. I would appreciate a hint. You've spent years training me to report verbatim, and I would like you to give a demonstration."

His head lifted and his eyes opened. "We're in a pickle."

"We have been for nearly a month. I need to know what Telesio said from the beginning."

"Nonsense. For an hour we merely prattled."

"Okay, that can wait. Then begin where he toasted Carla."

He did so. Once or twice I suspected him of skipping and stopped him, but on the whole I was willing to accept it as an adequate job. When he was through he reached for his glass and drank. I let my head back to rest on my clasped hands, and so was looking down my nose at him.

"On account of the wine," I said, "I may be a little vague, but it looks as if we have three choices. One, stay here and get nowhere. Two, go home and forget it. Three, go to Montenegro and get killed. I have never seen a less attractive batch to pick from."

"Neither have I." He put his glass down and took his watch from his vest pocket. "It's half-past seven, and I'm empty. I'll see what's in the kitchen." He arose and went for the door through which Telesio had gone for the wine and almonds. I followed. It certainly would not have qualified as a kitchen with the *Woman's Home Companion* or *Good Housekeeping,* but there was an electric stove with four units, and the pots and pans on hooks were clean and bright. Wolfe was opening cupboard doors and muttering something to himself about tin cans and civilization. I asked if I could help, and he said no, so I went and got my bag and opened it, got the necessary articles for a personal hour in a bathroom, and then realized that I hadn't seen one. However, there was one, upstairs. There was no hot water. An apparatus in the corner was probably a water heater, but the instructions riveted to it needed a lot of words, and rather than call Wolfe to come up and decode, I made out without it. The cord of my electric shaver wouldn't plug into the outlet, and even if it had fitted there was no telling what it might do to the circuit, so I used my scraper.

When I went back downstairs the living room was dark, but I made it to the windows and got the curtains over them before turning on the lights. In the kitchen I found Wolfe concentrated on cuisine, with his shirt sleeves rolled up, under a bright light from a ceiling fixture, and the window bare. I had to mount a chair to arrange the curtain so there were no cracks, after making a suitable remark.

We ate at a little table in the kitchen. Of course there was no milk, and Wolfe said he wouldn't recommend the water from the faucet, but I took a chance on it. He stuck to wine. There was just one item on the menu, dished by him out of a pot. After three mouthfuls I asked him what it was. A pasta called *tagliarini*, he said, with anchovies, tomato, garlic, olive oil, salt and pepper from the cupboard, sweet basil and parsley from the garden, and Romano cheese from a hole in the ground. I wanted to know how he had found a hole in the ground, and he said—offhand, as if it were nothing—by his memory of local custom. Actually he was boiling with pride, and by the time I got up to dish my third helping I was willing to grant him all rights to it.

While I washed up and put away, Wolfe went upstairs with his bag. When he came down again to the living room he stood and looked around to see if someone had brought a chair his size during his absence, discovered none, went to the couch and sat, and drew in air clear down to the *tagliarini* he had swallowed.

"Have we made up our mind?" I inquired.

"Yes."

"That's good. Which of the three did we pick?"

"None. I'm going to Montenegro, but not as myself. My name is Toné Stara, and I'm from Galichnik. You have never heard of Galichnik."

"Right."

"It is a village hanging to a mountain near the top, just over the border from Albania in Serbia, which is a part of Yugoslavia. It is forty miles southeast of Cetinje and the Black Mountain, and it is famous. For eleven months of each year only women live there—no men but a few in their dotage—and young boys. It has been that way for centuries. When the Turks seized Serbia more than five hundred years ago, groups of artisans in the lowlands fled to the mountains with their families, thinking the Turks would soon be driven out. But the Turks stayed, and as the years passed, the refugees, who had established a village on a crag and named it Galichnik, realized the hopelessness of wresting a living from the barren rocks. Some of the men, skilled craftsmen, started the practice of going to other lands, working for most of a year, and returning each July to spend a month at home with their women and children. The practice became universal with the men of Galichnik, and they have followed it for five centuries. Masons and stonecutters from Galichnik worked on the Escorial in Spain and the palaces at Versailles. They have worked on the Mormon Temple in Utah, the Château Frontenac in Quebec, the Empire State Building in New York, the Dnieperstroi in Russia."

He joined his fingertips. "So I am Toné Stara of Galich-

nik. I am one of the few who one July did not return—
many years ago. I have been many places, including the
United States. Finally I became homesick and curious.
What was happening to my birthplace, Glichnik, perched
on the border between Tito's Yugoslavia and Russia's pup-
pet Albania? I was eaten by a desire to see and to know,
and I returned. The answer was not in Galichnik. There
were no men there, and the women suspected me and
feared me and wouldn't even tell me where the men were. I
wanted to learn and to judge, as between Tito and the Russians, and between them both and certain persons of whom
I had vaguely heard, persons who were calling themselves
champions of freedom. So I made my way north through
the mountains, a hard rocky way, and here I am in Montenegro, determined to find out where the truth is and who
deserves my hand. I assert my right to ask questions so I
may choose my side."

He turned his palms up. "And I ask questions."

"Uh-huh." I wasn't enthusiastic. "I don't. I can't."

"I know you can't. Your name is Alex."

"Oh, It is,"

"It is if you go with me. There are good reasons why it
would be better for you to stay here, but confound it,
you've been too close to me too long. I'm too dependent
on you. However, the decision is yours. I don't claim the
right to drag you into a predicament of mortal hazard and
doubtful outcome."

"Yeah. I'm not very crazy about the name Alex. Why
Alex?"

"We can choose another. It might not increase the risk
of exposure for you to keep Archie, and that would make
one less demand on our vigilance. You are my son, born
in the United States. I must ask you to suffer that presump-
tion because no lesser tie would justify my hauling you
back to Galichnik with me. You are an only child and your
mother died in your infancy. That will reduce the tempta-
tion for you to indulge your invention if we meet someone
who speaks English. Until recently I repressed all sentiment about my homeland, so I have taught you no Serbo-
Croat and no Serbian lore. At one point, while I was cooking, I decided you should be a deaf-mute, but changed my
mind. It would create more difficulties than it would solve."

"It's an idea," I declared. "Why not? I practically am
anyway."

"No. You would be overheard talking with me."

"I suppose so," I conceded reluctantly. "I'd like to take a crack at it, but I guess you're right. Are we going to Galichnik?"

"Good Heavens, no. There was a time when sixty kilometers through those hills was only a frolic for me, but not now. We'll go across to a spot I used to know, or, if time has changed that too, to one that Paolo—"

The phone rang. I was up automatically, realized I was disqualified, and stood while Wolfe crossed to it and lifted it to his ear. In a moment he spoke, so it was Telesio. After a brief exchange he hung up and turned to me.

"Paolo. He has been waiting for Guido to return from an excursion on his boat. He said he might have to wait until midnight or later. I told him we have decided on a plan and would like to have him come and discuss it. He's coming."

I sat down. "Now about my name . . ."

VI

There are boats and boats. The *Queen Elizabeth* is a boat. So was the thing I rowed one August afternoon on the lake in Central Park, with Lily Rowan lolling in the stern, to win a bet. Guido Battista's craft, which took us across the Adriatic, was in between those two but was a much closer relative of the latter than of the former. It was twelve meters long, thirty-nine feet. It had not been thoroughly cleaned since the days when the Romans had used it to hijack spices from Levantine bootleggers, but had been modernized by installing an engine and propeller. One of my occupations en route was trying to figure out exactly where the galley slaves had sat, but it was too much for me.

We shoved off at three p.m. Monday, the idea being to land on the opposite shore at midnight or not long after. That seemed feasible until I saw the *Cispadana*, which was her name. To expect that affair to navigate 170 miles of open water in nine hours was so damn fantastic that I could make no adequate remark and so didn't try. It took her nine hours and twenty minutes.

Wolfe and I had stuck to the stuccoed hideout, but it had been a busy night and day for Telesio. After listening

48

to Wolfe's plan, opposing it on various grounds, and finally giving in because Wolfe wouldn't, he had gone again for Guido and brought him, and Wolfe and Guido had reached an understanding. Telesio had left with Guido, and I suppose he got a nap somewhere, but before noon Monday he was back with a carload. For me to choose from he had four pairs of pants, three sweaters, four jackets, an assortment of shirts, and five pairs of shoes; and about the same for Wolfe. They weren't new, except the shoes, but they were clean and whole. I picked them more for fit than looks, and ended up with a blue shirt, maroon sweater, dark green jacket, and light gray pants. Wolfe was tastier, with yellow, brown, and dark blue.

The knapsacks weren't new either, and none too clean, but we wiped them out and went ahead and packed. At the first try I was too generous with socks and underwear and had to back up and start over. In between roars of laughter, Telesio gave me sound advice: to ditch the underwear entirely, make it two pairs of socks, and cram in all the chocolate it would hold. Wolfe interpreted the advice for me, approved it, and followed it himself. I had expected another squabble about armament, but quite the contrary. In addition to being permitted to wear the Marley in the holster, I was provided with a Colt .38 that looked like new, and fifty rounds for it. I tried it in my jacket pocket, but it was too heavy, so I shifted it to my hip. I was also offered an eight-inch pointed knife, shiny and sharp, but turned it down. Telesio and Wolfe both insisted, saying there might be a situation where a knife would be much more useful than a gun, and I said not for me because I would be more apt to stick myself than the foe. "If a knife is so useful," I challenged Wolfe, "why don't you take one yourself?"

"I'm taking two," he replied; and he did. He put one in a sheath on his belt, and strapped a shorter one to his left leg just below his knee. That gave me a better idea of the kind of party we were going to, since in all the years I had known him he had never borne any weapon but a little gold penknife. The idea was made even clearer when Telesio took two small plastic tubes from his pocket and handed one to Wolfe and one to me. Wolfe frowned at it and asked him something, and they talked.

Wolfe turned to me. "He says the capsule inside the tube is a lullaby—a jocose term, I take it, for cyanide. He said for an emergency. I said we didn't want them. He said that

49

last month some Albanians, Russian agents, had a Montenegrin in a cave on the border for three days and left him there. When his friends found him the joints of all his fingers and toes had been broken, and his eyes had been removed, but he was still breathing. Paolo says he can furnish details of other incidents if we want them. Do you know what to do with a cyanide capsule?"

"Certainly. Everybody does."

"Where are you going to carry it?"

"My God, give me a chance. I never had one before. Sew it inside my sweater?"

"Your sweater might be gone."

"Tape it under my armpit."

"Too obvious. It would be found and taken."

"Okay, it's your turn. Where will you carry yours?"

"In my handiest pocket. Threatened with seizure and search, in my hand. Threatened more imminently, the capsule out of the tube and into my mouth. It can be kept in the mouth indefinitely if it is not crushed with the teeth. The case against carrying it is the risk of being stampeded into using it prematurely."

"I'll take the chance." I put the tube in my pocket. "Anyway, if you did that you'd never know it, so why worry?"

The lullabies completed our equipment.

It was considered undesirable for Telesio to be seen delivering us at the waterfront, so we said good-by there, with the help of a bottle of wine, and then he took us in the Fiat to the center of town, let us out, and drove away. We walked a block to a cab stand. I guess we weren't half as conspicuous as I thought we were, but the people of Bari didn't have the basis for comparison that I had. To think of Wolfe as I knew him best, seated in his custom-built chair behind his desk, prying the cap from a bottle of beer, a *Laeliocattleya Jaquetta* sporting four flowers to his left and a spray of *Dendrobium nobilius* to his right; and then to look at him tramping along in blue pants, yellow shirt, and brown jacket, with a blue sweater hanging over his arm and a bulging old knapsack on his back—I couldn't help being surprised that nobody turned to stare at him. Also, in that getup, I regarded myself as worth a glance, but none came our way. The hackie showed no sign of interest when we climbed into his cab and Wolfe told him where to go. His attitude toward obstacles was somewhat similar to Telesio's, but he got us into the old city and through its narrow winding streets to the edge of a wharf without making contact. I paid him and followed Wolfe out, and had my first view of the *Cispadana* sitting alongside the wharf.

Guido, standing there, left a man he was talking to and came to Wolfe. Here where he belonged he looked more probable than in the pink living room. He was tall, thin except his shoulders, and stooped some, and moved like a cat. He had told Wolfe he was sixty years old, but his long hair was jet black. The hair on his face was gray and raised questions. It was half an inch long. If he never shaved why wasn't it longer? If he did shave, when? I would have liked to ask him after we got acquainted, but we weren't communicating.

Telesio had said that with the three hundred bucks I had forked over he would take care of everything—our equipment, Guido, and a certain waterfront party—and apparently he had. I don't know what kind of voyage it was supposed to be officially, but no one around seemed to be interested. A couple of characters stood on the wharf and watched as we climbed aboard, and two others untied us and shoved the bow off when Guido had the engine going and gave the sign, and we slid away. I supposed one or both of them would jump on as we cleared, but they didn't. Wolfe and I were seated in the cockpit.

"Where's the crew?" I asked him.

He said Guido was the crew.

"Just him?"

"Yes."

"Good God. I'm not a mariner. When the engine quits or something else, who steers?"

"I do."

"Oh. You *are* a mariner."

"I have crossed this sea eighty times." He was working at the buckle of a knapsack strap. "Help me get this thing off."

My tongue was ready with a remark about a man of action who had to have help to doff his knapsack, but I thought I'd better save it. If the engine did quit, and a squall hit us, and he saved our lives with a display of masterly seamanship, I'd have to eat it.

Nothing happened at all the whole way. The engine was noisy, but that was all right; the point was, it never stopped being noisy. No squall. Late in the afternoon clouds began coming over from the east, and a light wind started up, but not enough to curl the water. I even took a nap, stretched out on a cockpit seat. A couple of times, when Guido went forward on errands, Wolfe took the wheel, but there was no call for seamanship. The third time was an hour before sundown, and Wolfe went and propped himself on the narrow board, put a hand on the wheel, and was motionless, looking ahead. Looking that way, the water was blue, but looking back, toward the low sun over Italy, it was gray except where the sun's rays bounced out of it at us. Guido was gone so long that I stepped down into the cabin to see what was up, and found him stirring something in an old black pot on an alcohol stove. I couldn't ask him what, but a little later I found out, when he appeared with a pair of battered old plates heaped with steaming spaghetti smothered with sauce. I had been wondering, just to myself, about grub. He also brought wine, naturally, and a tin pail filled with green salad. It wasn't quite up to Wolfe's production the day before, but Fritz himself wouldn't have been ashamed of the salad dressing, and it was absolutely a meal. Guido took the wheel while Wolfe and I ate, and then Wolfe went back to it and Guido went to the cabin to eat. He told us he didn't like to eat in the open air. Having smelled the inside of the cabin, I could have made a comment but didn't. By the time he came out it was getting dark, and he lighted the running lights before he went back to the wheel. The clouds had scattered around, so there were spaces with stars, and Guido began to sing and kept it up. With all the jolts I had had the past two days, I wouldn't have been surprised if Wolfe had joined in, but he didn't.

It had got pretty chilly, and I took off my jacket, put on the sweater, and put the jacket back on. I asked Wolfe if he didn't want to do the same, and he said no, he would soon be warming up with exercise. A little later he asked what time it was, my wristwatch having a luminous dial, and I told him ten past eleven. Suddenly the engine changed its tune, slowing down, and I thought uh-huh, I knew it, but it kept going, so evidently Guido had merely throttled down. Soon after that he spoke to Wolfe, and Wolfe went to the wheel while Guido went to douse the lights and then returned to his post. There wasn't a glimmer anywhere on the boat. I stood up to look ahead, and I have damn good eyes, but I had just decided that if there should be anything ahead I wouldn't see it anyway, when I saw something pop up to shut off a star.

I turned to Wolfe. "This is Guido's boat, and he's running it, but we're headed straight for something big."

"Certainly we are. Montenegro."

I looked at my watch. "Five after twelve. Then we're on time?"

"Yes." He didn't sound enthusiastic. "Will you please help me with this thing?"

I went and helped him on with his knapsack and then got mine on. After a little the engine changed tune again, slower and much quieter. The thing ahead was a lot higher and had spread out at the sides, and it kept going up. When it was nearly on top of us Guido left the wheel, ran in and killed the engine, came out and glided around the cabin to the bow, and in a moment there was a big splash. He came gliding back and untied the ropes that lashed the dinghy to the stern. I helped him turn the dinghy over, and we slid it into the water and pulled it alongside. This maneuver had been discussed on the way over, and Wolfe had informed me of the decision. On account of the displacement of Wolfe's weight, it would be safer for Guido to take him ashore first and come back for me, but that would take an extra twenty minutes and there was an outside chance that one of Tito's coast-guard boats would happen along, and if it did, not only would Guido lose his boat but also he would probably never see Italy again. So we were to make it in one trip. Guido held the dinghy in, and I took Wolfe's arm to steady him as he climbed over the side, but he shook me off, made it fairly neatly, and lowered himself in the stern. I followed and perched in the bow. Guido stepped down in the middle, light as a feather, shipped the oars, and rowed. He muttered something, and Wolfe spoke to me in an undertone.

"We have twelve centimeters above water amidships—about five inches. Don't bounce."

"Aye, aye, sir."

Guido's oars were as smooth as velvet, making no sound at all in the water and only a faint squeak in the rowlocks, which were just notches in the gunwale. As I was riding backward in the bow—and not caring to twist around for a look, under the circumstances—the news that we had made it came to me from Wolfe, not much above a whisper.

"Your left hand, Archie. The rock."

I saw no rock, but in a second there it was at my elbow, a level slab a foot above the gunwale. Flattening my palm on its surface, I held us in and eased us along until Guido could reach it too. Following the briefing I had been given, I climbed out, stretched out on the rock on my belly, extended a hand for Guido to moor to, and learned that he had a healthy grip. As we kept the dinghy snug to the rock, Wolfe engineered himself up and over and was towering above me. Guido released his grip and shoved off, and the dinghy disappeared into the night. I scrambled to my feet.

I had been told not to talk, so I whispered, "I'm turning on my flashlight."

"No."

"We'll tumble in sure as hell."

"Keep close behind me. I know every inch of this. Here, tie this to my sack."

I took his sweater, passed a sleeve under the straps, and knotted it with the other sleeve. He moved across the slab of rock, taking it easy, and I followed. Since I was three inches taller I could keep straight behind and still have a view ahead, though it wasn't much of a view, with the only light from some scattered stars. We stepped off the level slab onto another that sloped up, and then onto one that sloped down. Then we started up again, with loose coarse gravel underfoot instead of solid rock. When it got steeper Wolfe slowed up, and stopped now and then to get his breath. I wanted to warn him that he could be heard breathing for half a mile and therefore we might as well avoid a lot of stumbles by using a light, but decided it would be bad timing.

The idea was to get as far inland as possible before daylight, because we were supposed to have come north through the mountains from Galichnik, and then west toward Cetinje, and therefore it was undesirable to be seen near the coast. Also there was a particular spot about ten miles in, southeast of Cetinje, where we wanted to get something done before dawn. Ten miles in four hours was only a lazy stroll, but not in the dark across mountains, with Wolfe for a pacemaker.

He developed several annoying habits. Realizing that we were at the crest of a climb before I did, he would stop so abruptly that I had to brake fast not to bump into him. He would stumble going uphill but not down, which was unconventional, and I decided he did it just to be eccentric. He would stand still, with his head tilted back and swiveling from side to side, for minutes at a time, and when we were well away from the coast and undertones were permitted and I asked him what for, he muttered, "Stars. My memory has withered." The implication was that he was steering by them, and I didn't believe it. However, there were signs that he knew where he was; for instance, once at the bottom of a slope, after we had traveled at least eight miles, he turned sharply right, passed between two huge boulders where there was barely room for him, picked a way among a jungle of jagged rocks, stopped against a wall of rock that went straight up, extended his hands to it, and bent his head. Sound more than sight told me what he was doing; he had his hands cupped under a trickle of water coming down, and was drinking. I took a turn at it too and found it a lot better than what came from the faucet in Bari. After that I quit wondering if we were lost and just roaming around for the exercise.

No hint of dawn had shown when, on a fairly level stretch, he decelerated until he was barely moving, finally stopped, and turned and asked what time it was. I looked at my wrist and said a quarter past four.

"Your flashlight," he said. I drew it from a loop on my belt and switched it on, and he did the same with his. "You may have to find this spot without me," he said, "so you'd better take it in." He aimed his light to the left down a slope. "That one stone should do it—curled like the tail of a rooster. Put your light on it. There's no other like it between Budva and Podgorica. Get it indelibly."

It was thirty yards away, and I approached over rough ground for a better look. Jutting up to three times my height, one corner swept up in an arc, and it did resemble a rooster's tail if you wanted to use your fancy. I moved my light up and down and across, and, using the light to return to Wolfe, saw that we were on a winding trail.

"Okay," I told him. "Where?"

"This way." He left the trail in the other direction and soon was scrambling up a steep slope. Fifty yards from the trail he stopped and aimed his light up at a sharp angle. "Can you make it up to that ledge?"

It looked nearly perpendicular, twenty feet above our heads. "I can try," I said rashly, "if you stand where you'll cushion me when I fall."

"Start at the right." He pointed. "There. Kneeling on the ledge, the crevice will be about at your eye level, running horizontally. As a boy I used to crawl inside it, but you can't. It slopes down a little from twelve inches in. Put it in as far as you can reach, and poke it farther back with your flashlight. When you come to retrieve it you'll have to have a stick to fork it out with. You must bring the stick along because you won't find one anywhere near here."

As he talked I was opening my pants and pulling up my sweater and shirt to get at the money belt. Preparations for this performance had been made at Bari, wrapping the bills, eight thousand dollars of them, in five tight little packages of oilskin, and putting rubber bands around them. I stuffed them into my jacket pockets and took off my knapsack.

"Call me Tensing," I said, and went to the point indicated and started up. Wolfe changed positions to get a better angle for me with his light. I hooked my fingertips onto an inch-wide rim as high as I could reach, got the edge of my sole on another rim two feet up, and pulled, and there was ten per cent of it already done. The next place for a foot was a projecting knob, which I made with no trouble, but then my foot slipped off and I was back at the bottom.

Wolfe spoke. "Take off your shoes."

"I am," I said coldly. "And socks."

It wasn't too bad that way, just plenty bad enough. The ledge, when I finally made it, was at least ten inches wide. I called down to him, "You said to kneel. You come up and kneel. I'd like to see you."

"Not so loud," he said.

By clinging to a crack with one hand I managed to get the packages from my pockets with the other and push them into the crevice as far as my arm would go, and to slip the flashlight from its loop and shove them back. Getting the flashlight back into the loop with one hand was impossible, and I put it in a jacket pocket. I twisted my head to look at the way back and spoke again.

"I'll never make it down. Go get a ladder."

"Hug it," he said, "and use your toes."

Of course it was worse than going up—it always is—but I made it. When I was on his level again he growled, "Satisfactory." Not bothering to reply, I sat down on a rock and played the flashlight over my feet. They weren't cut to the bone anywhere, just some bruises and scratches, and no real flow of blood. There was still some skin left on most of the toes. Putting my socks and shoes on, I became aware that my face was covered with sweat and reached for my handkerchief.

"Come on," Wolfe said.

"Listen," I told him. "You wanted to get that lettuce cached before dawn, and it's there. But if there's any chance that I'll be sent to get it alone, we'd better not go on until daylight. I'll recognize the rooster's tail, that's all right, but how will I find it if I've traveled both approaches in the dark?"

"You'll find it," he declared. "It's only two miles to Rijeka, and a trail all the way. I should have said *very* satisfactory. Come on."

He moved. I got up and followed. It was still pitch dark. In half a mile I realized that we were hitting no more up-grades; it was all down. In another half a mile it was practically level. A dog barked, not far off. There was space around us—my eyes had accommodated to the limit, but I felt it rather than saw it—and underfoot wasn't rock or gravel, more like packed earth.

A little farther on Wolfe stopped, turned, and spoke. "We've entered the valley of the Moracha." He turned on his flashlight and aimed it ahead. "See that fork in the trail? Left joins the road to Rijeka. We'll take it later; now we'll find a place to rest." He turned the light off and moved. At the fork he went right.

This was according to plan as disclosed to me. There was no inn at Rijeka, which was only a village, and we were looking for a haystack. Ten minutes earlier we would have had to use the flashlights to find one, but now, as the trail became a road, there was suddenly light enough to see cart ruts, and in another hundred paces Wolfe turned left into a field, and I followed. The dim outline of the haystack was the wrong shape, but it was no time to be fussy, and I circled to the side away from the road, knelt, and started pulling out handfuls. Soon I had a niche deep enough for Wolfe. I asked him, "Do you wish to eat before going to your room?"

"No." He was grim. "I'm too far gone."

"A bite of chocolate would make a new man of you."

"No. I need help."

I got erect and helped him off with his knapsack. He removed his jacket, got into his sweater, put the jacket back on, and down he went—first to one knee, then both, then out flat. Getting into the niche was more than a simple rolling operation, since its mattress of hay was a good eight inches above ground level, but he made it.

"I'll take your shoes off," I offered.

"Confound it, no! I'd never get them on again!"

"Okay. If you get hungry ask for room service." I knelt to go to work on another niche, and made it long enough to stow the knapsacks at my head. When I was in and had myself arranged, facing outward, I called to Wolfe, "There's a faint pink glow in the east across the valley, ten miles away, above the Albanian Alps. Swell scenery."

No reply. I shut my eyes. Birds were singing.

VII

My first daylight view of Montenegro, some eight hours later, when I rolled out of the niche and stepped to the corner of the haystack, had various points of interest. Some ten miles off my port bow as I stood, a sharp peak rose high above the others. It had to be Mount Lovchen, the Black Mountain, so that was northwest, and the sun agreed. To the east was the wide green valley, and beyond it more mountains, in Albania. To the south, some two hundred yards off, was a clump of trees with a house partly showing. To the southwest was Nero Wolfe. He was in his niche, motionless, his eyes wide open, glaring at me.

"Good morning," I told him.

"What time is it?" he demanded. He sounded hoarse.

I looked at my wrist. "I should have said afternoon. Twenty to two. I'm hungry and thirsty."

"No doubt." He closed his eyes and in a moment opened them again. "Archie."

"Yes, sir."

"It is not a question of muscles. My legs ache, of course, and my back; indeed, I ache all over; but that was to be expected and can be borne. What concerns me is my feet. They carry nearly a hundredweight more than yours; they have been pampered for years; and I may have abused them beyond tolerance. They must be rubbed, but I dare not take off my shoes. They are dead. My legs end at my knees. I doubt if I can stand, and I couldn't possibly walk. Do you know anything about gangrene?"

"No, sir."

"It occurs in the extremities when there is interference with both arterial and venous circulation, but I suppose the interference must be prolonged."

"Sure. Eight hours wouldn't do it. I'm hungry."

He shut his eyes. "I awoke to a dull misery, but it is no

58

longer dull. It is overwhelming. I have been trying to move my toes, but I can't get the slightest sensation of having toes. The idea of squirming out of here and trying to stand up is wholly unacceptable. In fact, no idea whatever is acceptable other than asking you to pull my feet out and take off my shoes and socks; and that would be disastrous because I would never get them back on."

"Yeah. You said that before." I moved nearer. "Look, you might as well face it. This time stalling won't help. For years you've been talking yourself out of pinches, but it won't work on sore feet. If you can't walk there's no use trying. Tomorrow or next maybe, to prevent gangrene. Meanwhile there's a house in sight and I'll go make a call. How do you say in Serbo-Croat, 'Will you kindly sell me twenty pork chops, a peck of potatoes, four loaves of bread, a gallon of milk, a dozen oranges, five pounds—' "

Unquestionably it was hearing words like pork and bread that made him desperate enough to move. He did it with care. First he eased his head and shoulders out until he had his elbows on the ground, and then worked on back until his feet slid out. Stretched out on his back, he bent his right knee and then his left, slowly and cautiously. Nothing snapped, and he started to pump, at first about ten strokes a minute, then gradually faster. I had moved only enough to give him room, thinking it advisable to be at hand when he tried standing up, but I never had to touch him because he rolled over to the haystack and used it for a prop on his way up. Upright, he leaned against it and growled, "Heaven help me."

"It's you, O Lord. Amen. Is that the Black Mountain?"

He turned his head. "Yes. I never thought to see it again." He turned his back on it and was facing in the direction of the house in the clump of trees. "Why the devil weren't we disturbed long ago? I suppose old Vidin is no longer alive, but someone owns this haystack. We'll go and see. The knapsacks?"

I got them from my niche, and we started for the road, which was only a cart track. Wolfe's gait could not have been called a stride, but he didn't actually totter. The track took us to the edge of the clump of trees, and there was the house, of gray rock, low and long, with a thatched roof and only two small windows and a door in the stretch of stone. Off to the right was a smaller stone building with no windows at all. It looked a little grim, but not grimy. There was no sign of life, human or otherwise. A path of flat stones led to the door, and Wolfe took it. His first knock got no response, but after the second one the door opened about two inches and a female voice came through. After Wolfe exchanged a few noises with the voice the door closed.

"She says her husband is in the barn," he told me. "This is preposterous. I heard a rooster and goats." He started across the yard toward the door of the other building, and when we were halfway there it opened and a man appeared. He shut the door, stood with his back against it, and asked what we wanted. Wolfe told him we wanted food and drink and would pay for it. He said he had no food and only water to drink. Wolfe said all right, we would start with water, told me to come, and led the way over to a well near a corner of the house. It had a rope on a pulley, with a bucket at each end of the rope. One bucket, half full, was on the curb. I poured it into the trough, hauled up a fresh bucket, filled a cup that was there on a flat stone, and handed it to Wolfe. We each drank three cupfuls, and he reported on his talk with our host.

"It's worse than preposterous," he declared, "it's grotesque. Look at him. He resembles old Vidin some and may be a relative. In any case, he is certainly Montenegrin. Look at him. Six feet tall, a jaw like a rock, an eagle's beak for a nose, a brow to take any storm. In ten centuries the Turks could never make him whine. Even under the despotism of Black George he kept his head up as a man. But Communist despotism has done for him. Twenty years ago two strangers who had damaged his haystack would have been called to account; today, having espied us in trespass on his property, he tells his wife to stay indoors and shuts himself in the barn with his goats and chickens. Do you know how Tennyson addressed Tsernagora—the Black Mountain?"

"No."

"The last three lines of a sonnet:

"Great Tsernagora, never since thine own
    Black ridges drew the cloud and broke the storm
    Has breathed a race of mightier mountaineers."

He scowled in the direction of the mighty mountaineer standing at the barn door. "Pfui! Give me a thousand dinars."

While I was getting the roll from my pocket—procured for us by Telesio in Bari—I didn't need to figure how much

60

I was shelling out because I already had it filed that a thousand dinars was $3.33. Wolfe took it and approached our host. His line as later reported:

"We pay you for the damage to your haystack, which you can repair in five minutes. We also pay you for food. Have you any oranges?"

He looked startled, suspicious, wary, and sullen, all at once. He shook his head. "No."

"Any coffee?"

"No."

"Bacon or ham?"

"No. I have nothing at all."

"Bosh. If you think we are spies from Podgorica, or even Belgrade, you are wrong. We are——"

The man cut in. "You must not say Podgorica. You must say Titograd."

Wolfe nodded. "I am aware that the change has been made, but I haven't made up my mind whether to accept it. We have returned recently from the world outside, we are politically unattached, and we are starving. If necessary, my son, who is armed, can engage you while I enter the barn and get chickens—we would need two. It would be simpler and more agreeable for you to take this money and have your wife feed us. Have you any bacon or ham?"

"No."

"Something left of a kid?"

"No."

Wolfe roared, "Then what the devil have you?"

"Some sausage, of a sort." He hated to admit it. "A few eggs perhaps. Bread, and possibly a little lard."

Wolfe turned to me. "Another thousand dinars." I produced it, and he proffered it, with its twin, to our host. "Here, take it. We're at your mercy—but no lard. I overate of lard in my youth, and the smell sickens me. Your wife might conceivably find a little butter somewhere."

"No." He had the dough. "Butter is out of the question."

"Very well. That would pay for two good meals in the best hotel in Belgrade. Please bring us a pan, a piece of soap, and a towel."

He moved, in no hurry, to the house door and inside. When he came out again he had the articles requested. Wolfe put the metal pan, which was old and dented but clean, on the stone curb of the well, poured it half full of water, took off his jacket and sweater, rolled up his sleeves, and washed. I followed suit. The water was so cold it

61

numbed my fingers, but I was getting used to extreme hardship. The gray linen towel, brought ironed and folded, was two feet wide and four feet long when opened up. After I had got our combs and brushes from the knapsacks, and they had been used and repacked, I poured fresh water in the pan, placed it on the ground, sat on the edge of the well curb, took off my shoes and socks, and put a foot in the water. Stings and tingles shot through every nerve I had. Wolfe stood gazing down at the pan.

"Are you going to use soap?" he asked wistfully.

"I don't know. I haven't decided."

"You should have rubbed them first."

"No." I was emphatic. "My problem is different from yours. I lost hide."

He sat on the curb beside me and watched while I paddled in the pan, one foot and then the other, dried them with gentle pats of the towel, put on clean socks and my shoes, washed the dirty socks, and stretched them on a bush in the sun. When I started to wash the pan out he suddenly blurted, "Wait a minute. I think I'll risk it."

"Okay. I guess you could probably make it to Rijeka barefooted."

The test was never made because our host appeared and spoke, and Wolfe got up and headed for the door of the house, and I followed. The ceiling of the room we entered wasn't as low as I had expected. The wallpaper was patterned in green and yellow, but you couldn't see much of it on account of the dozens of pictures, all about the same size. There were rugs on the floor, carved chests and chairs with painted decorations, a big iron stove, and one small window. By the window was a table with a red cloth, with two places set—knives and forks and spoons and napkins. Wolfe and I went and sat, and two women came through an arched doorway. One of them, middle-aged, in a garment apparently made of old gray canvas, aimed sharp black eyes straight at us as she approached, bearing a loaded tray. The other one, following, made me forget how hungry I was for a full ten seconds. I didn't get a good view of her eyes because she kept them lowered, but the rest of her boosted my rating of the scenery of Montenegro more than the Black Mountain had.

When they had delivered the food and left I asked Wolfe, "Do you suppose the daughter wears that white blouse and embroidered green vest all the time?"

He snorted. "Certainly not. She heard us speaking a

foreign tongue, and we paid extravagantly for food. Would a Montenegrin girl miss such a chance?" He snorted again. "Would any girl? So she changed her clothes."

"That's a hell of an attitude," I protested. "We should appreciate her taking the trouble. If you want to take off your shoes, go ahead, and we can rent the haystack by the week until the swelling goes down."

He didn't bother to reply. Ten minutes later I asked him, "Why do they put gasoline in the sausage?"

At that, it wasn't a bad meal, and it certainly was needed. The eggs were okay, the dark bread was a little sour but edible, and the cherry jam, out of a half-gallon crock, would have been good anywhere. Someone told Wolfe later that in Belgrade fresh eggs were forty dinars apiece, and we each ate five, so we weren't such suckers. After one sip I gave the tea a miss, but there was nothing wrong with the water. As I was spreading jam on another slice of bread our host entered and said something and departed. I asked Wolfe what. He said the cart was ready. I asked, what cart? He said to take us to Rijeka.

I complained. "This is the first I've heard about a cart. The understanding was that you report all conversations in full. You have always maintained that if I left out anything at all you would never know whether you had the kernel or not. Now that the shoe's on the other foot, if you'll excuse my choice of metaphor, I feel the same way."

I don't think he heard me. His belly was full, but he was going to have to stand up again and walk, and he was too busy dreading it to debate with me. As we pushed back our chairs and got up, the daughter appeared in the arch and spoke, and I asked Wolfe, "What did she say?"

"*Sretan put.*"

"Please spell it."

He did so.

"What does it mean?"

"Happy going."

"How do I say, 'The going will be happier if you come along'?"

"You don't." He was on his way to the door. Not wanting to be rude, I crossed to the daughter and offered a hand, and she took it. Hers was nice and firm. For one little flash she raised her eyes to mine and then dropped them again. "Roses are red," I said distinctly, "violets are blue, sugar is sweet, and so are you." I gave her hand a gentle squeeze and tore myself away.

Out in the yard I found Wolfe standing with his arms folded and his lips compressed, glaring at a vehicle that deserved it. The horse wasn't so bad—undersized, nearer a pony than a horse, but in good shape—but the cart it was hitched to was nothing but a big wooden box on two iron-rimmed wheels. Wolfe turned to me.

"He says," he said bitterly, "that he put hay in it to sit on."

I nodded. "You'd never reach Rijeka alive." I went and got the knapsacks and our sweaters and jackets, and my socks from the bush. "It's only a little over a mile, isn't it? Let's go."

VIII

To build Rijeka all they had to do was knock off chunks of rock, roll them down to the edge of the valley, stack them in rectangles, and top the rectangles with thatched roofs; and that was all they had done, about the time Columbus started across the Atlantic to find India. Mud from the April rains was a foot deep in the one street, but there was a raised sidewalk of flat stones on either side. As we proceeded along it, single file, Wolfe in the lead, I got an impression that we were not welcome. I caught glimpses of human forms ahead, one or two on the sidewalk, a couple of children running along the top of a low stone wall, a woman in a yard with a broom; but they all disappeared before we reached them. There weren't even any faces at windows as we went by. I asked Wolfe's back, "What have we got, fleas?"

He stopped and turned. "No. They have. The sap has been sucked out of their spines. Pfui."

He went on. A little beyond the center of the village he left the walk to turn right through a gap in a stone wall into a yard. The house was set back a little farther than most of them, and was a little wider and higher. The door was arched at the top, with fancy carvings up the sides. Wolfe raised a fist to knock, but before his knuckles touched, the door swung open and a man confronted us.

Wolfe asked him, "Are you George Bilic?"

"I am." He was a low bass. "And you?"

"My name is unimportant, but you may have it. I am Toné Stara, and this is my son Alex. You own an automobile, and we wish to be driven to Podgorica. We will pay a proper amount."

Bilic's eyes narrowed. "I know of no place called Podgorica."

"You call it Titograd. I am not yet satisfied with the change, though I may be. My son and I are preparing to commit our sympathy and our resources. Of you we require merely a service for pay. I am willing to call it Titograd as a special favor to you."

"Where are you from and how did you get here?"

"That's our affair. You need merely to know that we will pay two thousand dinars to be driven twenty-three kilometers—or six American dollars, if you prefer them."

Bilic's narrow eyes in his round puffy face got narrower. "I do not prefer American dollars and I don't like such an ugly suggestion. How do you know I own an automobile?"

"That is known to everyone. Do you deny it?"

"No. But there's something wrong with it. A thing on the engine is broken, and it won't go."

"My son Alex will make it go. He's an expert."

Bilic shook his head. "I couldn't allow that. He might damage it permanently."

"You're quite right." Wolfe was sympathetic. "We are strangers to you. But I also know that you have a telephone, and you have kept us standing too long outside your door. We will enter and go with you to the telephone, and you will make a call to Belgrade, for which we will pay. You will get the Ministry of the Interior. Room Nineteen, and you will ask if it is desirable for you to cooperate with a man who calls himself Toné Stara—describing me, of course. And you will do this at once, for I am beginning to get a little impatient."

Wolfe's bluff wasn't as screwy as it sounds. From what Telesio had told him, he knew that Bilic would take no risk either of offending a stranger who might be connected with the secret police, or calling himself to the attention of headquarters in Belgrade by phoning to ask a dumb question. The bluff not only worked; it produced an effect which seemed to me entirely out of proportion when Wolfe told me later what he had said. Bilic suddenly went as pale as if all his blood had squirted out under his toenails. Simultaneously he tried to smile, and the combination wasn't attractive. "I beg your pardon, sir," he said in a different tone, backing up a step and bowing. "I'm sure you'll understand that it is necessary to be careful. Come in and sit down, and we'll have some wine."

"We haven't time." Wolfe was curt. "You will telephone at once."

"It would be ridiculous to telephone." Bilic was doing his best to smile. "After all, you merely wish to be driven to Titograd, which is natural and proper. Won't you come in?"

"No. We're in a hurry."

"Very well. I know what it is to be in a hurry, I assure you." He turned and shouted, "Jubé!"

He might just as well have whispered it, since Jubé had obviously been lurking not more than ten feet away. He came through a curtained arch—a tall and bony youth, maybe eighteen, in a blue shirt with open collar, and blue jeans he could have got from Sears Roebuck.

"My son is on vacation from the university," Bilic informed us. "He returns tomorrow to learn how to do his part in perfecting the Socialist Alliance of the Working People of Yugoslavia under the leadership of our great and beloved President. Jubé, this is Mr. Toné Stara and his son Alex. They wish to be driven to Titograd, and you will—"

"I heard what was said. I think you should telephone the Ministry in Belgrade."

Jubé was a complication that Telesio hadn't mentioned. I didn't like him. To get his contribution verbatim I would have to wait until Wolfe reported, but his tone was nasty, and I caught the Yugoslav sounds for "telephone" and "Belgrade," so I had the idea. It seemed to me that Jubé could do with a little guidance from an elder, and luckily his father felt the same way about it.

"As I have told you, my son," Bilic said sternly, "the day may have come for you to do your own thinking, but not mine. I think these gentlemen should be conveyed to Titograd in my automobile, and, since I have other things to do, I think you should drive them. If you regard yourself as sufficiently mature to ignore what I think, we can discuss the matter later in private, but I hereby instruct you to drive Mr. Stara and his son to Titograd. Do you intend to follow my instruction?"

They exchanged gazes. Bilic won. Jubé's eyes fell, and he muttered, "Yes."

"That is not a proper reply to your father."

"Yes, sir."

66

"Good. Go and start the engine."

The boy went. I shelled out some Yugoslav currency.

Bilic explained that the car would have to leave the village by way of the lane in the rear, on higher ground than the street, which the mud made impassable, and conducted us through the house and out the back door. If he had more family than Jubé, it kept out of sight. The grounds back of the house were neat, with thick grass and flowerbeds. A walk of flat stones took us to a stone building, and as we approached, a car backed out of it to the right, with Jubé at the wheel. I stared at it in astonishment. It was a 1953 Ford sedan. Then I remembered an item of the briefing Wolfe had given me on Yugoslavia: we had lent them, through the World Bank, a total of fifty-eight million bucks. How Bilic had managed to promote a Ford for himself out of it was to some extent my business, since I paid income tax, but I decided to table it. As we climbed in, Wolfe asked Bilic to inform his son that the trip had been fully paid for—two thousand dinars—and Bilic did so.

The road was level most of the way to Titograd, across the valley and up the Moracha River, but it took us more than an hour to cover the twenty-three kilometers—fourteen miles to you—chiefly on account of mud. I started in the back seat with Wolfe, but after the springs had hit in a couple of chuckholes I moved up front with Jubé. On the smooth stretches Wolfe posted me some on Titograd—but, since Jubé might have got some English at the university, he was Toné Stara telling his American-born son. As Podgorica, it had long been the commercial capital of Montenegro. Its name had been changed to Titograd in 1950. Its population was around twelve thousand. It had a fine old Turkish bridge across the Moracha. A tributary of the Moracha separated the old Turkish town, which had been inhabited by Albanians thirty years ago and probably still was, from the new Montenegrin town, which had been built in the latter half of the nineteenth century.

Twisted around in the front seat, I tried to deduce from Jubé's profile whether he knew more English than I did Serbo-Croat, but there was no sign one way or the other.

The commercial capital of Montenegro was a letdown. I hadn't expected a burg of twelve thousand to be one of the world's wonders, and Wolfe had told me that, under the Communists, Montenegro was still a backwater—but hadn't they changed the name to Titograd, and wasn't Tito the Number One? So, as we jolted and bumped over holes in the pavement and I took in the old gray two-story buildings that didn't even have thatched roofs to give them a tone, I felt cheated. I decided that if and when I became a dictator I would damn well clean a town up and widen some of its streets and have a little painting done before I changed its name to Goodwingrad. I had just made that decision when the car rolled to the curb and stopped in front of a stone edifice a lot bigger and some dirtier than most of those we had been passing.

Wolfe said something with an edge on his voice. Jubé turned in the seat to face him and made a little speech. For me the words were just a noise, but I didn't like his tone or his expression, so I slipped my hand inside my jacket to scratch myself in the neighborhood of my left armpit, bringing my fingers in contact with the butt of the Marley.

"No trouble, Alex," Wolfe assured me. "As you know, I asked him to leave us at the north end of the square, but he is being thoughtful. He says it is required that on arriving at a place travelers must have their identification papers inspected, and he thought it would be more convenient for us if he brought us here, to the local headquarters of the national police. Will you bring the knapsacks?"

He opened the door and was climbing out. Since the only papers we had with us were engraved dollars and dinars, I had a suspicion that his foot condition had affected his central nervous system and paralyzed his brain, but I was helpless. I couldn't even stop a passer-by and ask the way to the nearest hospital, and I had never felt so useless and so goddam silly as, with a knapsack under each arm, I followed Jubé and Wolfe across to the entrance and into the stone edifice. Inside, Jubé led us along a dim and dingy corridor, up a flight of stairs, and into a room where two men were perched on stools behind a counter. The men greeted him by name, not with an visible enthusiasm.

"Here are two travelers," Jubé said, "who wish to show their papers. I just drove them from Rijeka. I can't tell you how they got to Rijeka. The big fat one says his name is Toné Stara, and the other is his son Alex."

"In one respect," Wolfe objected, "that statement is not accurate. We do not wish to show papers, for an excellent reason. We have no papers to show."

"Hah!" Jubé cried in triumph.

One of the men said reasonably, "Merely the usual papers, nothing special. You can't live without papers."

"We have none."

68

"I don't believe it. Then where are they?"

"This is not a matter for clerks," Jubé declared. "Tell Gospo Stritar, and I'll take them in to him."

Either they didn't like being called clerks, or they didn't like Jubé, or both. They gave him dirty looks and exchanged mutterings, and one of them disappeared through an inner door, closing it behind him. Soon it opened again, and he stood holding it. I got the impression that Jubé was not specifically included in the invitation to pass through, but he came along, bringing up the rear.

This room was bigger but just as dingy. The glass in the high narrow windows had apparently last been washed the day the name had been changed from Podgorica to Titograd, four years ago. Of the two big old desks, one was unoccupied, and behind the other sat a lantern-jawed husky with bulging shoulders, who needed a haircut. Evidently he had been in conference with an individual in a chair at the end of the desk—one younger and a lot uglier, with a flat nose and a forehead that slanted back at a sharp angle from just above the eyebrows. The husky behind the desk, after a quick glance at Wolfe and me, focused on Jubé with no sign of cordiality.

"Where did you get these men?" he demanded.

Jubé told him. "They appeared at my father's house, from nowhere, and asked to be driven to Podgorica. The big fat one said Podgorica. He said he would pay two thousand dinars or six American dollars. He knew we have an automobile and a telephone. When his request was refused he told my father to telephone the Ministry of the Interior in Belgrade, Room Nineteen, and ask if he should cooperate with a man calling himself Toné Stara. My father thought it unnecessary to telephone, and commanded me to drive them to Titograd. On the way they talked together in a foreign tongue which I don't know but which I think was English. The big fat one told me to let them out at the north end of the square, but I brought them here instead, and now I am fully justified. They admit they have no papers. It will be interesting to hear them explain."

Jubé pulled a chair around and sat down. The husky eyed him. "Did I tell you to be seated?"

"No, you didn't."

"Then get up. I said get up! That's better, little man. You go to the university in Zagreb, that is true, and you have even spent three days in Belgrade, but I have not heard that you have been designated a hero of the people.

69

You did right to bring these men here, and I congratulate you on behalf of our great People's Republic, but if you try to assert yourself beyond your years and your position you will undoubtedly get your throat cut. Now go back home and study to improve yourself, and give my regards to your worthy father."

"You are being arbitrary, Gospo Stritar. It would be better for me to stay and hear—"

"Get out!"

I thought for a second the college boy was going to balk, and he did too, but the final vote was no. He turned and marched out. When the door had closed behind him, the one seated at the end of the desk got up, evidently meaning to leave, but Stritar said something to him, and he went to another chair and sat. Wolfe went and took the one at the end of the desk, and I took the one that Jubé had vacated.

Stritar looked at Wolfe, at me, and back at Wolfe. He spoke. "What's this talk about your having no papers?"

"Not talk," Wolfe told him. "A fact. We have none."

"Where are they? What's your story? Who stole them?"

"Nobody. We had no papers. You will find our story somewhat unusual."

"I already find it unusual. You had better talk."

"I intend to, Mr. Stritar. My name is Toné Stara. I was born in Galichnik, and at the age of sixteen I began to follow the well-known custom of spending eleven months of the year elsewhere to earn a living. For seven years I returned to Galichnik each July, but the eighth year I did not return because I had got married in a foreign land. My wife bore a son and died, but still I did not return. I had abandoned my father's craft and tried other activities, and I prospered. My son Alex grew up and joined in my activities, and we prospered more. I thought I had cut all bonds with my native land, shed all memories, but when Yugoslavia was expelled from the Cominform six years ago my interest was aroused, and so was my son's, and we followed developments more and more closely. Last July, when Yugoslavia resumed relations with Soviet Russia and Marshal Tito made his famous statement, my curiosity became intense. I became involved in arguments, not so much with others as with myself. I tried to get enough reliable information to make a final and just decision about the right and the wrong and the true interest and welfare of the people of my birthland."

He nodded sidewise at me. "My son's curiosity was as
70

great as mine, and we finally concluded that it was impossible to judge from so great a distance. We couldn't get satisfactory information, and we couldn't test what we did get. I determined to come and find out for myself. I thought it best for me to come alone, since my son couldn't speak the language, but he insisted on accompanying me, and in the end I consented. Naturally there was some difficulty, since we could not get passports for either Albania or Yugoslavia, and we chose to go by ship to Naples and fly to Bari. Leaving our luggage—and papers and certain other articles—at Bari, we arranged, through an agent who had been recommended to me, for a boat to take us across to the Albanian coast. Landing at night near Drin, we made our way across Albania to Galichnik, but we discovered in a few hours that nothing was to be learned there and crossed the border back into Albania."

"At what spot?" Stritar asked.

Wolfe shook his head. "I don't intend to cause trouble for anyone who has helped us. I had been somewhat inclined to think that Russian leadership offered the best hope for the people of my native land, but after a few days in Albania I was not so sure. People didn't want to talk with a stranger, but I heard enough to give me a suspicion that conditions might be better under Tito in Yugoslavia. Also I heard something of a feeling that the most promising future was with neither the Russians nor Marshal Tito, but with an underground movement that condemned both of them, so I was more confused than when I had left my adopted country in search of the truth. All the time, you understand, we were ourselves underground in a way, because we had no papers. I had, of course, intended all along to visit Yugoslavia, and now I was resolved also to learn more of the movement which I was told was called the Spirit of the Black Mountain. I suppose you have heard of it?"

Stritar smiled, not with amusement. "Oh yes, I've heard of it."

"I understand it is usually called simply the Spirit. No one would tell me the names of its leaders, but from certain hints I gathered that one of them was to be found near Mount Lovchen, which would seem logical. So we came north through the mountains and managed to get over the border into Yugoslavia, and across the valley and the river as far as Rijeka, but then we felt it was useless to go on to Cetinje without better information. In my boyhood

71

I had once been to Podgorica to visit a friend named Grubo Balar." Wolfe turned abruptly in his chair to look at the flat-nosed young man with a slanting forehead, seated over toward the wall. "I noticed when I came in that you look like him, and thought you might be his son. May I ask, is your name Balar?"

"No, it isn't," Flat-nose replied in a low smooth voice that was barely audible. "My name is Peter Zov, if that concerns you."

"Not at all, if it isn't Balar." Wolfe went back to Stritar. "So we decided to come to Podgorica—which I shall probably learn to call Titograd if we stay in this country—first to try to find my old friend, and second to see what it is like here. Someone had mentioned George Bilic of Rijeka, with his automobile and telephone, and we were footsore, so we sought him out and offered him two thousand dinars to drive us here. You will want to know why, when Bilic didn't want to oblige us, I told him to telephone the Ministry of the Interior in Belgrade. It was merely a maneuver —not very subtle, I admit—which I used once or twice in Albania, to test the atmosphere. If he had telephoned, it would have broadened the test considerably."

"If he had telephoned," Stritar said, "you would now be in jail and someone would be on his way from Belgrade to deal with you."

"All the better. That would tell me much."

"Perhaps more than you want to know. You told Bilic to ask for Room Nineteen. Why?"

"To impress him."

"Since you just arrived in Yugoslavia, how did you know about Room Nineteen?"

"It was mentioned to me several times in Albania."

"In what way?"

"As the lair of the panther who heads the secret police, and therefore the center of power." Wolfe flipped a hand. "Let me finish. I told Jubé Bilic to take us to the north corner of the square, but when he brought us here instead I thought it just as well. You would soon have learned of our presence, from someone else if not from him, and it would be better to see you and tell you about us."

"It would be better still to tell me the truth."

"I have told you the truth."

"Bah. Why did you offer to pay Bilic in American dollars?"

"Because we have some."

72

"How many?"

"Oh, more than a thousand."

"Where did you get them?"

"In the United States. That is a wonderful country to make money, and my son and I have made our full share, but it does not know how to arrange for a proper concentration of power, and therefore there is too much loose talk. That's why we came here to find out. Who can best concentrate the power of the Yugoslavs—the Russians, or Tito, or the Spirit of the Black Mountain?"

Stritar cocked his head and narrowed his eyes. "This is all very interesting, and extremely silly. It occurs to me that of the many millions lent to Yugoslavia by the World Bank—that is to say, by the United States—only one little million is being spent in Montenegro, for a dam and power plant just above Titograd, not three kilometers from here. If the World Bank wanted to know if the money is being spent for the agreed purpose, might it not send some such man as you to look?"

"It might," Wolfe conceded. "But not me. I am not technically qualified, and neither is my son."

"You can't possibly expect me," Stritar asserted, "to believe your fantastic story. I admit that I have no idea what you do expect. You must know that, having no papers, you are subject to arrest and a thorough examination, which you would find uncomfortable. You may be Russian agents. You may, as I said, be agents of the World Bank. You may be foreign spies from God knows where. You may be American friends of the Spirit of the Black Mountain. You may even have been sent from Room Nineteen in Belgrade, to test the loyalty and vigilance of Montenegrins. But I ask myself, if you are any of those, why in the name of God are you not provided with papers? It's ridiculous."

"Exactly." Wolfe nodded approvingly. "It is a pleasure to meet with an intelligent man, Mr. Stritar. You can account for our having no papers only by assuming that my fantastic story is true, as indeed it is. As for arresting us, I don't pretend that we would be delighted to spend a year or two in jail, but it would certainly answer some of the questions we have been asking. As for what we expect, why not allow us a reasonable amount of time, say a month, to get the information we came for? I would know better than to make such a suggestion in Belgrade, but this is Montenegro, where the Turks clawed at the crags for centuries to no purpose, and it seems unlikely that my son and I will topple them. To show that I am being completely frank with you, I said that we have more than a thousand American dollars, but I carry very little of it and my son only a fraction. We have cached most of it, a considerable amount, in the mountains, and it is significant that the spot we chose is not in Albania but in Montenegro. That would seem to imply that we lean to Tito instead of the Russians—did you say something, Mr. Zov?"

Peter Zov, who had made a noise that could have been only a grunt, shook his head. "No, but I could."

"Then say it," Stritar told him.

"American dollars in the mountains must not go to the Spirit."

"There is that risk," Wolfe admitted, "but I doubt if they'll be found, and what I have heard of that movement makes it even more doubtful that we will favor it. You're a man of action, are you, Mr. Zov?"

"I can do things, yes." The low, smooth voice was silky.

"Peter has earned a reputation," Stritar said.

"A good thing to have." Wolfe came back to Stritar. "But if he has in mind prying out of us where the dollars are, it doesn't seem advisable. We are American citizens, and serious violence to us would be indiscreet; and besides, the bulk of our fortune is in the United States, beyond your reach unless you enlist our sympathy and support."

"What place in the United States?"

"That's unimportant."

"Is Toné Stara your name there?"

"It may be, or maybe not. I can tell you, I understand the kind of power that is typified by Room Nineteen, and it attracts me, but I prefer not to call its attention to my friends and associates in America. It might be inconvenient in case I decide to return and stay."

"You may not be permitted to return."

"True. We take that risk."

"You're a pair of fools."

"Then don't waste your time on us. All a fool can do in Montenegro is fall off a mountain and break his neck, as you should know. If I came back here to fulfill my destiny, and brought my son along, why make a fuss about it?"

Stritar laughed. It seemed to me a plain, honest laugh, as if he were really amused, and I wondered what Wolfe had said, but I had to wait until later to find out. Peter Zov didn't join in. When Stritar was through being amused he

74

looked at his wristwatch, gave me a glance—the eighth or ninth he had shot at me—and then frowned at Wolfe. "You are aware," he said, "that everywhere you go in Titograd, and everything you say and do, will get to me. This is not London or Washington, or even Belgrade. I don't need to have you followed. If I want you in an hour, or five hours, or forty, I can get you—alive or dead. You say you understand the kind of power that is typified by Room Nineteen. If you don't, you will. I am now permitting you to go, but if I change my mind you'll know it."

He sounded severe, so it came as a surprise to see Wolfe leave his chair, tell me to come, and head for the door. I picked up the knapsacks and followed. In the outer room only one of the clerks was left, and he merely gave us a brief look as we passed through. Not being posted on our status, I was half expecting a squad to stop us downstairs and collar us, but the corridor was empty. On the sidewalk we got a few curious glances from passers-by as we stood a moment. I noted that Bilic's 1953 Ford was gone.

"This way," Wolfe said, turning right.

The next incident gave me a lot of satisfaction, and God knows I needed it. In New York, where I belong and know my way around and can read the signs, I no longer get any great kick out of it when a hunch comes through for me, but there in Titograd it gave me a lift to find that my nervous system was on the job in spite of all the handicaps. We had covered perhaps a quarter of a mile on the narrow sidewalks, dodging foreigners of various shapes and sizes, turning several corners, when I got the feeling that we had a tail and made a quick stop and wheel.

After one sharp glance I turned and caught up with Wolfe and told him, "Jubé is coming along behind. Not accidentally, because when I turned he dived into a doorway. The sooner you bring me up to date, the better."

"Not standing here in the street, being jostled. I wish you were a linguist."

"I don't. Do we shake Jubé?"

"No. Let him play. I want to sit down."

He went on, and I tagged along. Every fifty paces or so I looked back, but got no further glimpses of our college-boy tail until we had reached a strip of park along the river bank. That time he sidestepped behind a tree that was too thin to hide him. He badly needed some kindergarten coaching. Wolfe led the way to a wooden bench at the edge of a graveled path, sat, and compressed his lips as he straightened his legs to let his feet rest on the heels. I sat beside him and did likewise.

"I would have supposed," he said peevishly, "that yours would be hardier."

"Yeah. Did you climb a precipice barefooted?"

He closed his eyes and sat and breathed. After a little his eyes opened, and he spoke. "The river is at its highest now. This is the Zeta; you see where it joins the Moracha. Over there is the old Turkish town. In my boyhood only Albanians lived there, and according to Telesio only a few of them have left since Tito broke with Moscow."

"Thanks. When you finish telling me about the Albanians, tell me about us. I thought people without papers in Communist countries were given the full treatment. How did you horse him? From the beginning, please, straight through."

He reported. It was a nice enough spot, with the trees sporting new green leaves, and fresh green grass that needed mowing, and patches of red and yellow and blue flowers; and with enough noise from the river for him to disregard the people passing by along the path.

When he had finished I looked it over a little and asked a few questions, and then remarked, "Okay. All I could do was watch to see if you reached in your pocket for the lullaby. Did Stritar sick Jubé on us?"

"I don't know."

"If he did he needs some new personnel." I looked at my wrist. "It's after six o'clock. What's next—look for a good haystack while it's daylight?"

"You know what we came to Podgorica for."

I crossed my legs jauntily to show that I could. "I would like to make a suggestion. Extreme stubbornness is all very well when you're safe at home with the chain-bolt on the door, and if and when we're back there, call it Podgorica if you insist. But here it wouldn't bust a vein for you to call it Titograd."

"These vulgar barbarians have no right to degrade a history and deform a culture."

"No, and they have no right to give two American citizens the works, but they can and probably will. You can snarl 'Podgorica' at them while they're making you over. Are we waiting here for something?"

"No."

"Shall I go tie Jubé to a tree?"

"No. Ignore him."

"Then why don't we go?"

"Confound it, my feet!"

"What they need," I said sympathetically, "is exercise, to stimulate circulation. After a couple of weeks of steady walking and climbing you won't even notice you have feet."

"Shut up."

"Yes, sir."

He closed his eyes. In a minute he opened them again, slowly bent his left knee, and got his left foot flat on the ground, then his right.

"Very well," he said grimly, and stood up.

IX

It was a two-story stone house on a narrow cobbled street, back some three hundred yards from the river, with a tiny yard in front behind a wooden fence that had never been painted. If I had been Yugoslavia I would have spent a fair fraction of the fifty-eight million from the World Bank on paint. We had covered considerably more than three hundred yards getting there because of a detour to ask about Grudo Balar at the house where he had lived years before in his youth—a detour, Wolfe explained, which we bothered to make only because he had mentioned Balar to Gospo Stritar. The man who answered the door to Wolfe's knock said he had lived there only three years and had never heard of anyone named Balar, so we crossed him off.

When the door was opened to us at the two-story house on the narrow cobbled street I stared in surprise. It was the daughter of the owner of the haystack who had changed her clothes in our honor. Then a double take showed me that this one was several years older and a little plumper, but otherwise she could have been a duplicate. Wolfe said something, and she replied and turned her head to call within, and in a moment a man appeared, replaced her on the threshold, and spoke in Serbo-Croat.

"I'm Danilo Vukcic. Who are you?"

I won't say I would have spotted him in a crowd, for he didn't resemble his Uncle Marko much superficially, but he was the same family all right. He was a little taller than Marko had been, and not so burly, and his eyes were set deeper, but his head sat exactly the same and he had the same wide mouth with full lips—though it wasn't Marko's mouth, because Marko had spent a lot of time laughing, and this nephew didn't look as if he had laughed much.

"If you would step outside?" Wolfe suggested.

"What for? What do you want?"

"I want to say something not for other ears."

"There are no ears in my house that I don't trust."

"I congratulate you. But I haven't tested them as you have, so if you'll oblige me?"

"Who are you?"

"One who gets messages by telephone. Eight days ago I received one saying, 'The man you seek is within sight of the mountain.' Four days ago I received another saying that a person I knew had died a violent death within sight of the mountain. For speedy communication at a distance the telephone is supreme."

Danilo was staring at him, frowning, not believing. "It's impossible." Then he shifted the stare and frown to me. "Who is this?"

"My associate who came with me."

"Come in." He sidestepped to make room. "Come in quickly." We passed through, and he shut the door. "No one is here but my family. This way." He took us through an arch into an inner room, raising his voice to call as he went, "All right, Meta! Go ahead and feed them!" He stopped and faced Wolfe. "We have two small children."

"I know. Marko was concerned about them. He thought you and your wife were competent to calculate your risks, but they were not. He wanted you to send them to him in New York. Ivan is five years old and Zosha three. It is not a question of trusting ears; they are old enough to babble, as you should know."

"Of course." Danilo went and shut a door and returned. "They can't hear us. Who are you?"

"Nero Wolfe. This is Archie Goodwin. Marko may have spoken of him."

"Yes. But I can't believe it."

Wolfe nodded. "That comes first, naturally, for you to believe. It shouldn't be too difficult." He looked around. "If we could sit?"

None of the chairs in sight met his specifications, but there were several that would serve his main purpose, to

78

get his weight off his feet. I wouldn't have known that the big tiled object in the corner was a stove if I hadn't had the habit of spending an hour or so each month looking at the pictures in the *National Geographic,* and I had also seen most of the other articles of furniture, with the exception of the rug. It was a beaut, with red and yellow roses as big as my head on a blue background. Only a vulgar barbarian would have dragged a chair across it, so I lifted one to place it so as to be in the group after Wolfe had lowered himself onto the widest one available.

"It should help," Wolfe began, "to tell you how we got here." He proceeded to do so, in full, going back to the day, nearly a month earlier, when the news had come that Marko had been killed. From first to last Danilo kept a steady gaze at him, ignoring me completely, making no interruptions. He was a good listener. When Wolfe got to the end and stopped, Danilo gave me a long hard look and then went back to Wolfe.

"It is true," he said, "that through my uncle Marko I have heard of Nero Wolfe and Archie Goodwin. But why should you go to such trouble and expense to get here, and why do you come to me?"

Wolfe grunted. "So you're not satisfied. I understand the necessity for prudence, but surely this is excessive. If I am an imposter I already know enough to destroy you—Marko's associates in New York, the messages to me through Paolo Telesio, the house in Bari where you have met Marko, a dozen other details which I included. Either I am already equipped as the agent of your doom, or I am Nero Wolfe. I don't understand your incredulity. Why the devil did you send those messages if you didn't expect me to act?"

"I sent only one. The first one, that Carla was here, was only from Telesio. The second, that the man you sought was here, was sent because Carla said to. The last, that she had been killed, I sent because she would have wanted you to know. From what Marko had told me of you, I had no idea that you would come. When he was alive you had refused to give any support to the Spirit of the Black Mountain, so why should we have expected help from you when he was dead? Am I supposed to believe you have come to help?"

Wolfe shook his head. "No," he said bluntly. "To help your movement on its merits, no. No blow for freedom should be discouraged or scorned, but in this remote mountain corner the best you can do is tickle the tyrant's toes and die for your pains. If by any chance you should succeed in destroying Tito, the Russians would swarm in from all sides and finish you. I came to get a murderer. For years I have made a living catching wrongdoers, murderers in particular, and I don't intend to let the one who killed Marko escape. I expect you to help me."

"The one who killed Marko is only a tool. We have larger plans."

"No doubt. So have I, but this is personal, and at least it rides in your direction. It may be useful to make it clear that your friends in distant places cannot be slaughtered with impunity. I offer no bribe, but when I get back to America I shall probably feel, as the executor of Marko's estate, that his associates in a project dear to him deserve sympathetic consideration."

"I don't believe you'll ever get back. This isn't America, and you don't know how to operate here. Already you have made five bad mistakes. For one thing, you have exposed yourselves to that baby rat, Jubé Bilic, and let him follow you here."

"But," Wolfe objected, "I was told by Telesio that it would place you in no danger if we were seen coming here. He said you are being paid by both Belgrade and the Russians, and you are trusted by neither, and neither is ready to remove you."

"Nobody trusts anyone," Danilo said harshly. He left his chair. "But this Jubé Bilic, for a Montenegrin, has at his age a fatal disease of the bones. Even Montenegrins like Gospo Stritar, who work for Tito and have his picture on their walls if not in their hearts, have only contempt for such as Jubé Bilic, who spies on his own father. Contempt is all right, that's healthy enough, but sometimes it turns into fear, and that's too much. Do I understand that Jubé followed you to this house?"

Wolfe turned to me. "He wants to know if Jubé followed us here."

"He did," I declared, "unless he stumbled and fell in the last two hundred yards. I saw him turn the corner into this street."

Wolfe relayed it. "In that case," Danilo said, "you must excuse me while I arrange something." He left the room through the door toward the back of the house, closing it behind him.

"What's up?" I asked Wolfe. "Has he gone to phone Room Nineteen?"

"Possibly." He was peevish. "Ostensibly he intends to do something about Jubé."

"Where are we?"

He told me. It didn't take long, since most of the long conversation had been Wolfe's explanation of our presence. I asked him what the odds were that Danilo was double-crossing the Spirit and actually earning his pay from either Belgrade or the Russians, and he said he didn't know but that Marko had trusted his nephew without reservation. I said that was jolly, since if Danilo was a louse it would be interesting to see which side he sold us to, and I could hardly wait to find out. Wolfe only growled, whether in Serbo-Croat or English I couldn't tell.

It was quite a wait. I got up and inspected various articles in the room, asking Wolfe some questions about them, and concluded that if I lived to marry and settle down, which at the moment looked like a bad bet, our apartment would be furnished with domestic products, with possibly a few imports to give it tone, like for instance the tasseled blue scarf that covered a table. I was looking at pictures on the wall when the door opened behind me, and I admit that as I about-faced my hand went automatically to my hip, where I still had the Colt .38. It was only Meta Vukcic. She came in a couple of steps and said something, and Wolfe replied, and after a brief exchange she went out. He reported, without being asked, that she had said that the lamb stew would be ready in about an hour, and meanwhile did we want some goat milk, or vodka with or without water, and he had said no. I protested that I was thirsty, and he said all right, then call her, though he knew damn well I didn't know how to say "Mrs."

I asked him. "How do you say 'Mrs. Vukcic'?" He made a two-syllabled noise without any vowels. I said, "To hell with it," went to the door at the rear, pulled it open, passed through, saw our hostess arranging things on a table, caught her eye, curved my fingers as if holding a glass, raised the glass to my mouth, and drank. She said something that ended with a question mark, and I nodded. While she got a pitcher from a shelf and poured white liquid from it into a glass, I glanced around, saw a stove with a covered pot on it, a bank of cupboards with flowers painted on the doors, a table set for four, a line of shiny pots and pans

81

hanging, and other items. When she gave me the glass I asked myself if it would be appropriate to kiss her hand, which was well shaped but a little red and rough, decided against it, and returned to the other room.

"I had a little chat with Mrs. Vukcic," I told Wolfe. "The stew smells good, and the table is set for four, but there are no place cards, so keep your fingers crossed."

Lily Rowan had once paid a Park Avenue medicine man fifty bucks to tell her that goat milk would be good for her nerves, and while she was giving it a whirl I had sampled it a few times, so the liquid Meta Vukcic had served me was no great shock. By the time I had finished it the room was dark, and I went and turned the switch on a lamp that stood on the tasseled blue table cover, and it worked.

The door opened, and Danilo was back with us, alone. He crossed to the chair facing Wolfe and sat.

"You must excuse me," he said, "for being away so long, but there was a little difficulty. Now. You said you expect me to help you. What kind of help?"

"That depends," Wolfe told him, "on the situation. If you can tell me the name of the man who killed Marko, and where he is, that may be all I'll need from you. Can you?"

"No."

"Don't you know?"

"No."

Wolfe's tone sharpened. "I must remind you that last Friday, four days ago, Josip Pasic took Telesio a message from you to the effect that he was to telephone me that the man I sought was within sight of the mountain. You sent that message?"

"Yes, but, as I told you, I sent it because Carla said to."

"She told you to send that message without telling you who the man was, and you didn't ask her? Pfui."

"I had no chance to ask her. You don't know the circumstances."

"I have come four thousand miles to learn them. I confidently expected you to name the man."

"I can't." Danilo was resentful. "I am accustomed to being regarded with suspicion by nearly everyone here, I invite it and I welcome it, but from you, my uncle's oldest and closest friend, who denied us your help, I would not expect it. Carla came eleven days ago—no, twelve, a week ago Friday. She did not come here to Titograd—like you, she had no papers, and, unlike you, she took precautions. She went to a place she knew of near the Albanian border,

82

in the mountains, and sent me word, and I went to her. I had certain urgent affairs here and could stay there only one day. Her purpose was to arrange matters that Marko, being dead, could no longer attend to, but she shouldn't have crossed the sea. She should have sent for me from Bari. That place in the mountains is at the center of danger. I tried to persuade her to return to Bari, but she wouldn't. You knew her."

"Yes, I knew her."

"She was too headstrong. I had to leave her there. Two days later, on Sunday, word came from her that I was to send you that message, and I sent—"

"Who brought it?"

"Josip Pasic. At the moment there was no one else to send across to Telesio in Bari, and I sent him. Affairs still kept me here, and I couldn't get away until Tuesday—that was a week ago today. I went to the mountains that night—it is always best to go at night—and Carla was not there. We found her body the next morning at the foot of a cliff. She had been stabbed in several places, but on account of the bruises from the fall down the cliff it was impossible to tell to what extent she had been mistreated. Anyway, she was dead. Because she had had no papers, and for other reasons, it would have been difficult to arrange Christian burial for her, but the body was decently disposed of. It would be a pleasure to tell you that we tracked those who had killed her and dealt with them, but it is not that simple in the mountains, and besides, there was another urgent concern—to take precautions regarding materials that must be guarded. It was possible that before killing her they had forced her to reveal the cache. We attended to that Wednesday night; and Thursday, Josip Pasic and I came back to Titograd; and that night he went to the coast and crossed to Bari, to send word to New York about Carla. I thought it proper also to tell Telesio to get word to you, since she was your daughter."

Danilo made a gesture. "So there it is. I hade no chance to ask her who killed Marko."

Wolfe regarded him glumly. "You had a chance to ask Josip Pasic."

"He doesn't know."

"He was in the mountains with her."

"Not precisely with her. She was trying to do something alone, against all reason."

"I want to see him. Where is he?"

"In the mountains. He returned there Saturday night."

"You can send for him."

"I can, of course, but I'm not going to." Danilo was emphatic. "The situation there is difficult, and he must stay. Besides, I won't expose Josip to the hazard of a meeting with you in Titograd, not after the way you have performed and made yourself conspicuous. Marching into the headquarters of the secret police! Walking the streets, anywhere you please, in daylight! It is true that Titograd is no metropolis, it is only a poor little town in this little valley surrounded by mountains, but there are a few people here who have been over the mountains and across the seas, and what if one of them saw you? Do you think I am such a fool as to believe you are Nero Wolfe just because you come to my house and say so? I would have been dead long ago. Once—last winter, it was—my uncle showed me a picture of you that had been printed in an American newspaper, and I recognized you as soon as I saw you at my door. There are others in Titograd who might also recognize you, but you march right in and tell Gospo Stritar you are Toné Stara of Galichnik!"

"I apologize," Wolfe said stiffly, "if I have imperiled you."

Danilo waved it away. "That's not it. The Russians know I take money from Belgrade, and Belgrade knows I take money from the Russians, and they both know I am involved with the Spirit of the Black Mountain, so no one can imperil me. I slip through everybody's fingers like quicksilver—or like mud, as they think. But not Josip Pasic. If I had him meet you in Titograd, and by some mischance— No. Anyway, he can't leave. Also, what can he tell you? If he knew— Yes, Meta?"

The door had opened, and Mrs. Vukcic had appeared. She came in a step and said something. Danilo, replying, arose, and so did Wolfe and I as she came toward us.

"I have told my wife who you are," Danilo said. "Meta, this is Mr. Wolfe and Mr. Goodwin. There is no reason why you shouldn't shake hands with them." She did so, with a firm, friendly clasp. Danilo went on, "I know, gentlemen, that, like my uncle, you are accustomed to the finest dishes and delicacies, but a man can only share what he has, and at least we'll have bread."

We certainly had bread. It was a very nice party. At the table in the kitchen an electric lamp with a big pink shade was between Wolfe and me so I couldn't see him without stretching my neck, but that was no great hardship. Mrs. Vukcic was a wonderful hostess. It never occurred to Wolfe or Danilo to give a damn whether I had any notion of what they were talking about, which I hadn't, but Meta couldn't stand a guest at her table feeling out of it, so about once a minute she turned her black eyes to me just to include me in. I was reminded of a dinner party Lily Rowan had once thrown at Rusterman's where one of the guests was an Eskimo, and I tried to remember whether she had been as gracious to him as Meta Vukcic was being to me, but I couldn't, probably because I had completely ignored him myself. I resolved that if I ever got back to New York and was invited to a meal where someone like an Eskimo was present, I would smile at him or her at least every fifth bite.

There was nothing wrong with the lamb stew, and the radishes were young and crisp, but the big treat was the bread, baked by Mrs. Vukcic in a loaf about as big around as my arm and fully as long. We finished two of them, and I did my part. There was no butter, but sopping in the gravy was taken for granted, and, when that gave out, the bread was even better with a gob of apple butter on each bite. It was really an advantage not being able to follow the conversation, since it kept me busy catering for myself and at the same time making sure I met Meta's glances to show proper appreciation; and anyway, when Wolfe reported later, he said the table talk was immaterial.

There was even coffee—at least, when I asked Wolfe about it, he said it was supposed to be. I won't dwell on it. We were all sipping away at it, out of squatty yellow cups, when suddenly Danilo left his chair, crossed to a door—not the one to the living room—opened it enough to slip through, and did so, closing the door behind him. In view of what followed, there must have been some kind of signal, though I hadn't heard or seen any. Danilo wasn't gone more than five minutes. When he re-entered he opened the door wider, and a breath of outdoor air came in, enough to get to us at the table. He came back to his chair, sat, put a wad of crumpled brown paper on the table, picked up his coffee cup, and emptied it. Wolfe asked him something in a polite tone. He put the cup down, picked up the wad of paper, unfolded it, got it straightened out, and placed it on the table between him and Wolfe. I stared at the object he had unwrapped, resting there on the paper. Though my eyes are good, at the first glance I didn't believe them, but when they checked it I had to. The object was a human finger that had been chopped off at the base, no question about it.

"Not for desert, I hope," Wolfe said dryly.

"It would be poison," Danilo declared. "It belonged to that baby rat, Jubé Bilic. Meta dear, could I have some hot coffee?"

She got up and went to the stove for the pot.

X

Meta did not seem to be shocked by the display of an unattached human finger on her dining table, but she was. The proof is that she filled her husband's cup with steaming so-called coffee and returned the pot to the stove without asking her guests if they wanted some, which was not like her. When she was back in her chair Wolfe spoke.

"An impressive exhibit, Danilo, no doubt of that. Naturally you expect a question, and I supply it. Where's the rest of him?"

"Where it won't be found." Danilo sipped. "This method of confirming a removal is not a Montenegrin custom, as you know. It was introduced to us by the Russians a few years ago, and we have indulged them by adopting it."

"It seems extreme—not the finger, the removal. I assume that when you left us you went to tell someone that he was lurking in this neighborhood, and to give instructions that he be found and removed."

"That's right."

Wolfe grunted. "Only because he had followed us to your house?"

"No." Danilo picked up the exhibit, wadded the paper around it, got up and went to the stove, opened the door, tossed the thing in, closed the door, and returned to his chair. "It will smell a little," he said, "but no more than a morsel of lamb. Jubé has been a nuisance ever since he started going to the university. For a year now he has made things harder for me by trying to persuade Gospo Stritar that my true loyalty is to the Spirit of the Black Mountain —and also, I have reason to believe, trying to persuade Belgrade. He was already condemned, and by following you here he merely presented an opportunity."

Wolfe lifted his shoulders an eighth of an inch and let them down. "Then it was no disservice to lead him here. I don't pretend that I'm not impressed by the dispatch and boldness with which you grasped the opportunity." His eyes moved to Meta. "And I assure you, Mrs. Vukcic, that the grotesque table decoration served with the coffee has not diminished our gratitude for an excellent meal. I speak for Mr. Goodwin too, because he has none of your words." He returned to Danilo and sharpened his tone. "If I may return to my affair? I must see Josip Pasic."

"He can't come," Danilo said bluntly.

"I ask you to reconsider."

"No."

"Then I'll have to go to him. Where is he?"

"That's impossible. I can't tell you."

Wolfe was patient. "You can't? Or you won't?"

"I'm not going to." Danilo put his hands flat on the table. "For the sake of my uncle, Mr. Nero Wolfe, I have shaken your hand and so has my wife, and we have shared bread with you. But for the sake of what he believed in and supported, I will not run the risk of betraying one of our most carefully guarded secrets. It is not necessary to question your good faith; your rashness is enough. You may already have been recognized."

Wolfe snorted. "In this outlandish getup? Nonsense. Besides, I have arranged for a diversion. Paolo Telesio communicates with you by mail, using this address, and those communications are intercepted by the secret police and inspected before they are delivered to you; and you and Telesio, knowing that, have occasionally taken advantage of it. Is that true?"

Danilo was frowning. "Apparently Paolo has higher regard for your discretion than I have."

"He knew me before you were born. Does the interception delay delivery to you considerably?"

"No. They work it fairly well."

"Did you get a letter from Telesio today?"

"No."

"Then tomorrow, I suppose. He mailed it in Bari yesterday afternoon. In it he tells you that he has just received a cablegram from New York, signed Nero Wolfe, reading as follows: 'Inform proper persons across Adriatic I am handling Vukcic's affairs and assuming obligations. Two hundred thousand dollars available soon. Will send agent conference Bari next month.' Telesio's letter will say that it came in English and he has put it in Italian. As I say, it is a diversion for the police. For you it has no validity. I promised Telesio I would make that plain. To the interceptors it should be plain that Nero Wolfe is in New York and has no intention of crossing an ocean."

Danilo, still frowning, objected, "Belgrade has people in New York. They'll learn you're not there."

"I doubt it. I rarely leave my house, and the man in my office, answering my telephone, named Saul Panzer, could flummox Tito and Molotov put together. There's another purpose the cablegram may possibly serve, but that's an off-chance. Now for Josip Pasic. I intend to see him. You spoke of the risk of betraying a carefully guarded secret, but if it's what I assume it is, I already know it. Marko never told me explicitly that weapons and ammunition were being smuggled in to you, but he might as well have. He said that certain costly and essential supplies were being stored at a spot in the mountains less than three kilometers from the place where I was born, and he identified the spot. We both knew it well in boyhood. It must have been near there that Carla was killed. It must be there, or nearby, that this Josip Pasic is so importantly engaged that you refuse to call him away. So my course is simple. I don't fancy spending another night cruising the mountains, and we'll stay the night in Titograd, heaven knows where, and go tomorrow. We shall betray no secrets heedlessly, but we have to find Pasic."

He pushed back his chair and stood up. "Thank you again, Mrs. Vukcic, for your hospitality. And you, Danilo, thank you for whatever you consider to deserve thanks." He switched to English. "If you'll get the knapsacks, Archie? We're leaving. What time is it?"

I looked at my wrist as I arose. "Quarter to ten."

"Sit down, you fools," Danilo growled.

Wolfe ignored it. "You can do us one more favor," he suggested. "Tell me, is there a hotel in town with good beds?"

"By God," Danilo growled. In Serbo-Croat "by God" is *"Boga ti"*—good for growling. Danilo repeated it. "By God, without papers, with nothing but money, you would go to a hotel! You'd get a good bed all right! Gospo Stritar is a man who is capable of a thought, or you would be in jail now, and not in bed either! He merely decided you would be more interesting loose, and by God he was correct! You tell me to my face you know where our cache is, and tomorrow in the sunshine, like going to a picnic, you will go there, doubtless to the very spot, and shout for Josip Pasic!"

He calmed down a little. "Only," he said, "you would be dead before you got there, and that would be nothing to regret. You may be fit to live in America, but not here. There are only twenty-two men in Montenegro who know where that cache is, and you two are not with us, so obviously you must die. Damn it, sit down!"

"We're going, Danilo."

"You can't go. While I was out I made other arrangements besides Jubé. There are men out front and out back, and if you leave and I don't go to the door with you and give a signal, you won't get far. Sit down."

Wolfe told me, "There's a snag, Archie," and sat, and I followed suit.

"I would like to say something, Danilo," Mrs. Vukcic said quietly.

He frowned at her. "Well?" he demaned.

She looked at Wolfe, at me, and back at her husband. "These men are not crazy like you and me," she told him. "They are not doomed like us. We try to pretend there is hope, but our hearts are dead, and we can only pray that someday there will be real life for Ivan and Zosha, but we know there can be none for us. Oh, I don't complain! You know I love you for fighting instead of giving in like the others, and I'm proud of you—I am, Danilo—but I don't want to be afraid of you. It is too easy for you to say these men must die, and it makes me afraid, because they are the only hope for Ivan and Zosha, men like them. I know you had to kill Jubé Bilic, I can understand that; but these men are our friends, or anyway they are the friends of our children. Do you love anybody?"

"Yes. I love you."

"And the children, I know. Do you love anybody else?"

"Who else would I love?"

She nodded, her black eyes flashing. "That's what I mean, you see? These men can still love people! They came so far, so many thousands of miles into danger, because they loved your Uncle Marko and they want to find the man who killed him. What else did they come for? All I want—I want you to understand that, and I know it isn't easy because it wasn't easy for me—we can't have that

89

kind of love, but we can understand it, and we can hope for Ivan and Zosha to grow up to have it someday. You can't just say these men must die."

"I can say whatever is necessary."

"But it isn't. And anyway, you didn't mean it. I know how you say a thing when you mean it. You must forgive me, Danilo, for speaking, but I was afraid you would go on like that until you couldn't back down. It made my heart stop beating to hear you say these men must die, because that is exactly wrong. The real truth is that these men must *not* die."

"Bah." He was scowling at her. "You talk like a woman."

"I talk like a mother, and if you think that is something no fine, brave man should listen to, I ask you, who made me a mother? You can't wipe it out now."

All I knew was that it was no longer a very nice party, and all I could do was watch their faces, including Wolfe's, and listen to their voices, and try to guess what was up. Also I had to keep an eye on Wolfe's left hand, because we had arranged that he would close his left fist and open it again if a conversation reached a point where I should be ready to join in with the Marley or the Colt. It was damned unsatisfactory. As far as I knew, Danilo might be scowling at his wife because she was begging him to stick a knife in me so she could have my green jacket to make over for Ivan and Zosha. I heard their names three times.

Wolfe put in, "You're in a fix, Danilo," he said sympathetically. "If you let us go we might unwittingly endanger your plans, I admit it. If you have us removed, you will affront the memory of Marko and all he did for you, and also, if you listen to your wife, you will forfeit your claim on the future. I suggest a compromise. You say it is always best to go there at night. Take us there now. If it is impossible for you to leave, get someone to take us. We will be as circumspect as occasion will permit."

"Yes, Danilo!" Meta cried. "That would be the best—"

"Be quiet," he commanded her. He leveled his deepset eyes at Wolfe. "It would be unheard of, to take strangers there."

"Pfui. A stranger to my own birthplace?"

"I'll take you to the coast instead, tonight, and arrange for you to cross to Bari. You can wait there for word from me. I promise to do all I can to find the man who killed Marko, and to deal with him."

"No. I have made a promise to myself that has priority, and I will not delegate it. Besides, if you failed I would have to come back; and anyway, if you sent me a finger how would I know who it had belonged to? No, Danilo. I will not be diverted."

Danilo got up, went to the stove, opened the door, and looked in at the fire. I suppose Wolfe's mention of a finger had reminded him that he had a cremation under way and he wanted to check. Apparently he thought it needed stoking, for he got some sticks of wood from a box and poked them in before he closed the door. Then he came and stood directly behind my chair. Since Wolfe's last words had sounded like an ultimatum, and since I didn't care for the idea of a knife in my back without even catching sight of it, I twisted around enough to get a glimpse of it on its way. His hands were buried in his pockets.

"You're barely able to stand up," he told Wolfe. "What about your feet?"

"I'll manage," Wolfe said without a quaver. "Must we walk the whole way?"

"No. We'll ride twenty kilometers along the Cijevna, as far as the road goes. From there it's rough and steep."

"I know it is. I herded goats there. Do we leave now?"

"No. Around midnight. I must go and make arrangements for a car and driver. Don't step outside while I'm gone."

He went. I must say for him that once he had accepted a situation he didn't waste any time bellyaching. As soon as the door had closed behind him I went at Wolfe.

"Now what? Has he gone for another finger?"

He said something to Meta, and she replied, and he pushed back his chair and stood up, flinching only a little. "We'll go in the other room," he told me, and moved, and I followed, leaving the door open, not to be rude to our hostess. He lowered himself onto his former chair, put his palms on his knees, and sighed as far down as it would go. "We're in for another night of it," he said glumly, and proceeded to report. First he sketched it, and then, when I insisted, filled it in. He was in no humor to oblige me or anyone else, but I was in no humor to settle for a skeleton.

When he had finished I sat a minute and turned it over. I had certainly seen sweeter prospects. "Is there such a thing," I asked, "as a metal dinar any more? A coin?"

"I doubt it. Why?"

"I'd like to have one to toss, to decide which side Danilo

is really on. I admit his wife thinks she knows, but does she? As it stands now, I could name at least fourteen people I would rather have take me for a ride than Marko's nephew."

"I am committed," he said grumpily. "You are not."

"Phooey. I want to see your birthplace and put a plaque on it."

No comment. He sighed again, arose from his chair, crossed to a sofa with a high back that was against the far wall, placed a cushion to suit him, and stretched out. He tried it first on his back, but protruded over the edge, and turned on his side. It was a pathetic sight, and to take my mind off it I went to another wall and looked at pictures some more.

I think he got a nap in. Some time later, when Danilo returned, I had to go to the sofa and touch Wolfe's arm before he would open his eyes. He gave me a dirty look, and one just as dirty to Danilo, swung his legs around, sat, and ran his fingers through his hair.

"We can go now," Danilo announced. He had on a leather jacket.

"Very well." Wolfe made it to his feet. "The knapsacks, Archie?"

As I bent to lift them Meta's voice came from the doorway. Her husband answered her, and Wolfe said something and then spoke to me. "Archie, Mrs. Vukcic asks if we would like to look at the children, and I said yes."

I kept my face straight. The day that Wolfe would like to climb steps to look at children will be the day I would like to climb Mount Everest barefooted to make a snowman. However, it was good public relations, and I don't deny he might have felt that we should show some appreciation for her contribution to the discussion of our future. I know I did, so I dropped the knapsacks and gave her a cordial smile. She led the way through the arch and up a flight of narrow wooden stairs, uncarpeted, with Wolfe and me following and Danilo bringing up the rear. On the top landing she murmured something to Wolfe, and we waited there while she disappeared through a doorway and in a moment rejoined us, carrying a lighted candle. After going to another door that was closed, she opened it gently and crossed the sill. With the heavy shoes we were wearing it wasn't easy to step quietly, and with the condition Wolfe's feet were in it wasn't easy for him to tiptoe, but by gum he tried, and made, on the bare floor, quite a little less noise than a team of horses.

They were in beds, not cribs, with high wooden posts, against opposite walls. Zosha, who was on her back, with one of her long black curls across her nose, had kicked the cover off, and Meta pulled it up. Wolfe, looking down at her, muttered something, but I can't say what because he has always refused to tell me. Ivan, who was on his side with an arm stretched out, had a smudge on his cheek, but you have to make allowance for the fact that when Meta put them to bed unexpected guests had arrived and she had been under pressure. When Meta turned away with the candle, and Wolfe and I followed, Danilo stayed by Ivan's bed, and we waited for him at the foot of the stairs, with Meta holding the candle high to light him.

In the living room Danilo spoke to Wolfe, and Wolfe relayed it to me. "We'll go first, by a route I know, not far, and Danilo will follow. We won't want the knapsacks on our backs in the car, so if you'll carry them?"

We shook hands with Meta. I picked up the luggage. Danilo escorted us to the front door and let us out, and we were loose again. It was past midnight and the houses were all dark, and so was the street, except for one dim excuse for a light at the corner a hundred yards away. We headed in the other direction. When we had gone some fifty paces I stopped and wheeled to look back, and Wolfe grumbled, "That's futile."

"Okay," I conceded, "but I trust Danilo as far as I can see him, and now I can't see him."

"Then why look? Come on."

I obeyed, with my arms full of knapsacks. There were some stars, and soon my eyes were adjusted enough for objects thirty feet off and for movements much farther. Before long we came to a dead end and turned left. At the next intersection we turned right, and in a few minutes went left again and were on a dirt road with ruts. There were no more houses, but ahead in the distance was a big black outline against the sky, and I asked Wolfe what it was.

"Sawmill. The car's there."

He sounded more confident than I felt, but he was right. When we approached the outline it became a building surrounded by other outlines, and closer up they became stacks of lumber. I saw the car first, off the road, in between the second and third stacks, which were twice as high as my head. We went up to it. It was a car all right, an old Chevvy sedan, and the hood was warm to my hand, but it was empty.

"What the hell," I said. "No driver? I have no road map."

"He'll come." Wolfe opened the rear door and was climbing in. "There'll be four of us, so you'll have to ride with me."

I put the knapsacks in, taking care not to drop them on his feet, but stayed out on the ground. With my hands free, I had a strong impulse to get the Marley in one and the Colt in the other, and I had to explain to myself why it would be a waste of energy. If someone not Danilo arrived I certainly wasn't going to shoot on sight, and I wouldn't even know what his viewpoint was until Wolfe interpreted for me. I compromised by transfering the Colt from my hip to my side pocket.

It was Danilo who arrived. Hearing footsteps, I looked around the corner of the lumber pile and saw him coming down the road. When he was close enough to recognize I took my hand out of my pocket, which shows the state of mind I was in. According to me, he was as likely to saw off our limb as anyone. He turned in, brushing past me, went to the car and spoke to Wolfe, turned, and pronounced a word that sounded something like Steven. Immediately a man appeared beside him, coming from above. He had jumped down from the lumber pile, where he had been perched, probably peeking down at me, while I had been talking myself out of drawing my guns.

"This is Stefan Protic," Danilo told Wolfe. "I have told him about you and your son Alex. Seen anything, Stefan?"

"No. Nothing."

"All right, we'll go."

Danilo got in with Wolfe, so I circled the car and climbed in beside Stefan. He gave me a long, hard, deliberate look, and I returned it as well as I could in the darkness. About all I could tell was that he was some shorter than me, with a long narrow face that certainly wasn't pale, and broad shoulders. He started the engine, which sounded as if it would appreciate a valve job, rolled into the road, and turned right, without turning his lights on.

I can't tell you anything about the first three miles, or five kilometers, of that ride, because I saw nothing. I had already suspected that European drivers had kinks that

94

nothing could be done about, and now concluded that Stefan's was an antipathy for lights, when suddenly he flashed them on, and I saw why we had been bumping so much. You couldn't have driven that road without bumping if it had been lined on both sides with continuous neons. I remarked over my shoulder, "If you'll tell this bird to stop I'd rather get out and run along behind."

I expected no reply but got one. Wolfe's voice came, punctuated by bumps. "The main routes from Podgorica are north and south. This is merely a lane to nowhere."

Podgorica again. Also he wasn't going to have me casting slurs at Montenegro, which was pretty generous of him, considering the kind of reception Montenegro was giving us.

In another mile or so the road smoothed off a little and started up and began to wind. Wolfe informed me that we were now along the Cijevna, and on our right, quite close, I caught glimpses of the white of a rushing stream, but the engine was too noisy for me to hear it. I remembered that one evening after dinner I had heard Wolfe and Marko discussing the trout they had caught in their early days, Marko claiming he had once landed one forty centimeters long, and I had translated it into inches—sixteen. I swiveled my head to ask Wolfe if it was in the Cijevna that he and Marko had got trout, and he said yes, but in a tone of voice that did not invite conversation, so I let it lay.

The road got narrower and steeper, and after a while there was no more Cijevna, anyhow not visible. Stefan shifted to second to negotiate a couple of hairpin turns, tried to get going in high again, couldn't make it, and settled for second. The air coming in my open window was colder and fresher, and in the range of our lights ahead there were no longer any leaves or grass, or anything growing; nothing but rock. I had seen no sign of a habitation for more than a mile, and was thinking that Wolfe must have been hatched in an eagle's nest, when suddenly space widened out in front of us, and right ahead, not fifty feet away, was a stone house, and the car stopped with a jerk. I was making sure it was really a house and not just more of the rock, when Stefan switched off the lights and everything was black.

Danilo said something, and we all piled out. I got the knapsacks. Stefan went toward the house, came back in a moment with a can, lifted the hood and removed the radiator cap, and poured water in. When that chore was finished he got in behind the wheel, got turned around with a lot of noisy backing and tacking, and was gone. Soon I was relieved to see, down below, his lights flash on.

Wolfe spoke. "My knapsack, Archie, if you please?"

XI

We got to Josip Pasic, according to the luminous dial on my wrist, at eighteen minutes past three in the morning. I did not, and still don't, understand how Wolfe ever made it. We didn't actually scale any cliffs—it was supposed to be a trail all the way except the last three hundred yards—but it was all up, and at least fifty times my hands had to help my feet. I must admit that Danilo was very decent about it. Even in the dark he could probably have romped along like a goat, but he would always wait like a gentleman for Wolfe to catch up. I had no choice. I was behind, and if Wolfe had toppled he would have taken me with him.

There was no taboo on talking, and during the halts Danilo did some briefing, and Wolfe passed it on to me when he had a little breath to spare. Our destination was not the cache but a decoy. The costly and essential supplies had been moved. There were guards at the new cache, but Pasic and five others were at the old one, now empty, expecting and awaiting an invasion. It sounded goofy to me, six guys sitting in a cave asking for it, but I understood it better when we got there.

The last three hundred yards, after we left the trail, were not the hardest but they were the most interesting. Danilo, saying that at one point we would have to walk a ledge less than a meter wide with a five-hundred-meter drop, had suggested that he bring Pasic to us at the trail, but Wolfe had vetoed it. When we got to the ledge, which was nearly level, apparently it meant nothing to him. As for me, I didn't spend my boyhood herding goats around cliffs and chasms, and I would have preferred to be walking down Fifth Avenue, or even Sixth. There was enough light from the stars to see the edge, and then nothing. Wide open spaces are okay fairly horizontal, but not straight down.

96

We were still on the ledge, at least I was, when Danilo stopped and uttered a word, raising his voice a little, and at once an answering voice came from up ahead. Our guide replied, "Danilo. Two men are with me, but I'll come on alone. You can use the light."

We had to stand there and wait on the damn ledge. When the beam of a spotlight hit us, after taking in Danilo, it was worse. The light left us and went back to Danilo, and then was turned off. In a moment voices came, not loud, and kept on, and my feeling for the Spirit of the Black Mountain took a dive. I admit it was in order for Danilo to explain us to his pals, but that ledge was one hell of an anteroom. Finally the light came at us again, and Danilo called to us to come. When we moved the light didn't attend us but stayed focused on the ledge. In a few steps we left it. I would have had to grope, but Wolfe didn't, and I realized it wasn't so much his eyes he steered by as his memory.

Two figures were standing in front of a black blotch on the dim face of perpendicular rock—the entrance to the cave. As we reached them Danilo gave us the name of Josip Pasic, and gave him ours—Nero Wolfe and Archie Goodwin. That had been accepted as unavoidable, since Danilo couldn't have justified bringing Toné Stara and his son Alex in to his friends, nor account for their interest in Carla. Pasic didn't offer a hand, and neither did Wolfe, who is allergic to handshaking anyhow. Danilo said he had told Pasic who we were and why we wanted to see him. Wolfe said he wanted to sit down. Danilo said there were blankets in the cave, but men were sleeping on them. I thought if it was me I would be under them. It was cold as the devil.

Pasic said, "Montenegrins sit on rocks."

We did so, after Pasic had turned off the spotlight, Wolfe and Danilo side by side on one, and Pasic and me facing them on another.

"What I want is simple," Wolfe said. "I want to know who killed Marko Vukcic. He was my oldest friend. As boys we often explored this cave. Danilo says you don't know who killed him."

"That's right. I don't."

"But nine days ago you took a message from Carla to Danilo that the man who killed him was here."

"That wasn't the message."

"That's what it meant. Please understand, Mr. Pasic, I have no desire or intention to try to badger you. I merely

97

want all the information you can give me about that message and the events behind it. Danilo will tell you I can be trusted with it."

"Carla was his daughter," Danilo said. "He has a certain right to know."

"I knew a man who had a daughter." Pasic was scornful. "So did you. She betrayed him to the police."

"That's another matter. I brought him here, Josip. I don't think the time has come for you to question your trust in me."

I was wishing I could have a good look at Pasic. He was just a blur, a big one, taller than me, with a tight, bitter voice. At first, sitting next to him, I had noticed that he smelled, and then had realized that it was me, after the sweat of the climb.

"All right," he said, "this is what happened. Carla came to the house—that's the house at the end of the road, where the car brought you. You saw the house?"

"Yes," Wolfe said. "I was born there."

"That's right, you were, I have been told. We didn't know she was coming, and it was a big surprise. She wanted to see Danilo, and I went and brought him. They talked a whole day. I don't know what they said because it was not thought desirable for me to be present."

"That's foolish," Danilo declared. "I told you what was said. Many things were said, but the main one was that Carla knew from Marko that we had reason to think there was a spy among us, and she wanted to know who. There are spies in the Spirit, of course, that is to be expected, but this one seemed to be close to our most secret affairs. Coming from a distance, Carla was right to exclude no one, not even you or me. She had to talk with someone, and she chose me. And as I told you, I didn't satisfy her."

"I know you didn't. Neither did I, when she talked with me after you left. She trusted none of us, and she died for it." Pasic moved his head, to Wolfe. "She decided to find the spy herself. Since you were born here, you know that it is only two kilometers from this spot to Albania, and that just across the border is an old Roman fort."

"Certainly. I've killed bats in it."

"There are no bats in it now. The Albanians, under the whip of the Russians, have cleaned it up some, and they like to stand in the tower and look across the border. For a while they kept a squad there, but now not so many. I had told Carla that if there was a spy among us working for

98

the Russians it would surely be known to the Albanians at the fort, and they would be in touch with them, and I'm sorry I told her that because it gave her the idea. She decided to go herself to the fort, go straight to them, and offer her services as a spy. I told her it was not only dangerous, it was absurd, but she wouldn't listen. If you think I should have kept her from going, you will please remember that in her mind it was possible that I was myself the spy. Besides, I would have had to restrain her physically. She had decided on it."

Wolfe grunted. "So she went."

"Yes. She went early Sunday morning. I couldn't keep her, but I persuaded her to make an arrangement with me. I knew how things were in the fort. There are places to sleep and a place to cook, but there is no plumbing. For private necessities there is only one place to go, a little room on the lower side that is more like a cell, with no light when the door is closed, because there is no window."

"I know that room."

"You seem to know everything. When you knew it, it was not furnished with a bench to sit on with holes in it."

"No."

"It is now. I figured that if Carla were left free to move at all, she would be allowed to go to that room. A few meters from it, on the other side of the corridor, is another room whose outer wall has crumbled, not used for anything—but of course you know that too. The arrangement was that I would be in that other room at nine o'clock that evening, and Carla would walk past it to the cell. That was all we arranged. We left it to circumstances whether she would enter the room to speak to me, or I would join her in the cell, or what. But she was to walk past the room unless it was absolutely impossible, as near nine o'clock as she could, for if she didn't I was going to find out why."

Pasic turned his head to cock an ear in the direction of the ledge, heard nothing whatever if my ears are any good, and turned back. He went on, "There is a thing I would like to mention, since you too are from America, where there is plenty of good food. There are still a few men in Montenegro with some pride, and I am one of them. On Saturday, after Carla arrived, I sent a man down to a farm in the valley and he brought back eight eggs and a piece of bacon. So Sunday morning before she left Carla had for breakfast three of the eggs and some slices of bacon, and she said it was better than American bacon. I want you to

99

know that her last meal in Montenegro was a good one."

"Thank you," Wolfe said courteously.

"You are welcome. Soon after she left—in fact, nearly on her heels—I sent a man, one named Stan Kosor, with a binocular. It is a very fine binocular with a long range, one of the many fine things we have received from America through Marko Vukcic. It has a name engraved on it, 'E. B. Meyrowitz,' which certainly does not seem to be an American name, but it came from America. Stan Kosor went to a high spot near the border, from which the fort is in plain view with the binocular, and stayed there all day. He is now in the cave asleep, and you can speak with him in the morning if you wish. He saw nothing out of the ordinary. No one arrived from the south—and, particularly, no one departed. Naturally I wanted to know if they took Carla toward Tirana, which is only a hundred and fifty kilometers away. I am trying to accommodate you. You said you wanted all the information I can give you about that message and the events behind it."

"Yes. Go ahead."

"There were four men here with me besides Stan Kosor. A little after dark Sunday evening we took the trail to the border, and Stan Kosor joined us there. He said he was sure that Carla was still at the fort. We took off our shoes before we went on, not so much on account of the men in the fort, who are merely Albanians, but because of the dog, which liked to lie after dark on a certain rock that is raised a little, at the corner nearest the trail. I left the men at a certain spot and approached alone, and had to climb and circle clear around the fort in order to come at the dog from the other direction, against the wind. That way I got to his rock and sank my knife in him before he moved or made a sound. I pulled his carcass out of the way behind a boulder, and stood a while to listen. I had seen lights at four windows, and I could hear voices, very faint, and I thought one of them was Carla's."

He stopped again to turn his ears toward the ledge, and, after ten seconds of the deadest silence I had ever listened to, turned back and resumed. "With the dog out of the way it was simple. I went around to where the wall had crumbled and climbed through a hole into the room where I was to wait. The door into the corridor was open a little, and I stood so I could see through. It wasn't nine o'clock yet. My plan was to wait until ten o'clock, and then, if she hadn't come, I was going to go and bring the men, and we would find her. Of course we would first have to deal with the Albanians, but that wouldn't take long because there wouldn't be more than four of them, and probably only two or three."

His hand moved in a quick little gesture. "You will permit me to confess something. I was hoping she would not come, and the Albanians would try to fight and would have to be killed, and we would find her locked in a room, unharmed. That way she would be back with us, and also some enemies would be dead. Of course we could go there and kill them any time, but I admit that would be useless, because, as Danilo says, others would come to take their place, who would give us more trouble than they do now. However, that is what I was hoping. It is not what happened. It was barely nine o'clock when I heard footsteps that sounded like Carla's, and then I saw her in the corridor, carrying a little lantern. I started to stick a hand through the opening for her to see, but pulled it back for fear she was being watched from the end of the corridor. She stopped right at the opening and turned to face the way she had come, and said my name in a whisper, and I answered. She said she was all right and she might come back tomorrow, and then she gave me that message, and—"

"If you don't mind," Wolfe put in, "try to remember the exact words."

"I don't have to try. She said, 'I'm all right, don't worry, I may come back tomorrow. Tell Danilo to send word to Nero Wolfe that the man he seeks is within sight of the mountain. Did you hear that?' I said, 'Yes.' She said, 'Do it at once, tonight. That's all, I must hurry.' She crossed the corridor and went in the little room and shut the door. Naturally I wanted to ask her things, but it was impossible to go and join her in the little room, both for reasons of decency and because it might have placed her in danger. I waited until I saw her come out and return down the corridor and turn a corner, and then I left. I returned to the others and put on my shoes, and we came back to the cave, and I went at once to Podgorica and told Danilo. Is that the information you wanted from me?"

"Yes. Thank you. You didn't see her again?"

"Not alive. Wednesday morning Danilo and I found her body. I would like to ask you something."

"Go ahead."

"I have been told that you are an expert detective, with

101

a great reputation for understanding things. In your opinion, am I responsible for Carla's death? Were they moved to kill her because I killed the dog?"

"That's silly, Josip," Danilo said gruffly. "I was in a temper when I said that. Can't you forget it?"

"He wants my opinion," Wolfe said. "It is this. Many men are responsible for Carla's death, but if I were to name one it would be Georgi Malenkov. He is the foremost champion of the doctrine that men and women must be subjected to the mandates of despotic power. No, Mr. Pasic, you cannot be held accountable, either for Carla's death or for the fact that your information forces me to undertake a distasteful errand. There's nothing else for it; I must go to that fort—that is, if I can walk in the morning." He started to rise, dropped back on the rock, and groaned as if he meant it. "By heaven, if I can stand up! Can you spare me a blanket, Danilo?"

He tried again and made it to his feet.

XII

I nearly froze.

There were no extra blankets. I suppose there would have been if the costly and essential supplies had not been moved to another cache, but that didn't keep me warm. Pasic gave Wolfe his blanket, and, being a proud Montenegrin with guests, offered to get one from one of the sleeping men for me, but I said oh no, I wouldn't think of it, through my interpreter. I spent the rest of the night—what was left—thinking of it. Wolfe had told me the elevation there was five thousand feet, but he must have meant meters. The pile of hay Pasic assigned me to was damp, and pulling some of it over me only made things worse. I guess I must have slept some, because I know I dreamed, something about a lot of dogs with cold noses.

I heard voices and opened my eyes and saw bright sunshine outside the cave entrance. My watch said ten past eight, so I had been refrigerating for more than four hours. I lay and figured it out: if I was frozen I couldn't move, so if I could move I wasn't frozen. I bent the legs and raised the torso, scrambled to my feet, and tottered to the entrance.

The sun wasn't there yet. To get it on me I would have

had to go to the ledge and out on it a way, and I was all through with that ledge if there was any other possible route out of there. Then I remembered; we weren't going back, but forward; we were going to cross the border to the old Roman fort to visit Albanians. Wolfe had explained it all to me before we had entered the cave to hit the hay, including Pasic's strategy with the dog. No doubt that had influenced my dream.

"Good morning," Wolfe said. He was sitting on a rock, looking exactly the way I felt.

If I reported all the details of the next hour you would think I was piling on the misery just for the hell of it, so I'll mention only a few to give you a notion. The sun stuck to a crazy slant so as not to touch us. There was water in a can to drink, but none to wash in. I was told that to wash all I had to do was go over the ledge to the trail and down it less than a kilometer to a brook. I didn't wash. For breakfast we had bread, nothing like Meta's, cold slices of mush that had been fried in lard, and canned beans from the United States of America. When I asked Wolfe why they didn't at least start a fire and make some tea, he said because there was nothing to burn, and, looking around, I had to admit he was right. There wasn't a single stick, alive or dead, anywhere in sight. Just rock. And of course I couldn't talk, which might have helped to get the blood started. There wasn't even anything to listen to, except the goddam jabber as usual. The five men whom I hadn't met formally kept off in a group, with their jabber pitched low, evidently, judging from their sidelong glances, discussing Wolfe and me. Wolfe and Danilo and Pasic had a long argument, won by Wolfe, though I didn't know that until later, when he told me they had opposed his announced plan so strongly they had even threatened to set up a trail block.

Then he started an argument with me and lost it. His idea was that he would stand a better chance with the Albanians if he went alone, because they would be much more reluctant to talk if there were two of us, and they would be particularly suspicious of one who couldn't speak Albanian, which was a different language from Serbo-Croat. Actually it wasn't an argument, because I didn't argue. I merely said flatly nothing doing, on the ground that there would be nothing at the cave for lunch but cold mush, and Pasic had said there was a place at the fort for cooking.

It wasn't until the knapsacks were strapped on and we were ready to go that I realized we would have to return to the trail by way of the ledge. Numb and dumb with cold, I had been supposing that we would go on to the border without any backtracking. With seven pairs of eyes on me, not counting Wolfe's, it was up to me to sustain the honor of American manhood, and I set my jaw and did my best. It helped that my back was to them. An interesting question about walking a narrow ledge over a fifteen-hundred-foot drop is whether it's better to do it at night or in the daytime. My answer is that it's better not to do it at all.

After we got to the trail it wasn't bad. The sun and the exercise were thawing me out, and there was no hard going. When we came to a rivulet crossing the trail we stopped and drank, and ate some chocolate. I told Wolfe it would take me only five minutes to rinse off my feet and put on fresh socks, and he said there was no great hurry, so I took off my knapsack and went to it. The water was like ice, but you can't have everything. Wolfe sat on a rock and chewed chocolate. He informed me that Albania was just ahead, about three hundred meters, but was unmarked because a debate had been going on for centuries as to the exact line of the water-parting in this section of the mountains. Also he pointed to a niche in a crag towering above us and said that was where Stan Kosor had perched with the binocular to watch the fort the day Carla had gone there. He added that almost certainly Kosor would be back in the niche today, to watch again. It was a perfect spot for it, since he could aim his glass at the fort through a crack.

I asked Wolfe how his feet were. "It is no longer merely my feet," he declared. "It is every muscle and nerve in my body. No words would serve, so I won't waste any."

It was warming up, so we took off our sweaters before going on. We crossed into Albania without knowing precisely when, and in another three minutes rounded a corner, and there was the fort. It was against a perpendicular wall of rock so high there was no point in straining my neck to find the top, and was of course a perfect match. Where the trail passed it there was a level space twenty yards wide and twice as long, and at its farther end a little brook splashed across the trail. There were slits in the walls, and in the one facing the trail the rock had crumbled to leave a big hole, presumably Pasic's point of entry for his appointment with Carla.

There was no sign of life, not even a dog. The idea was just to walk in and introduce ourselves, announcing, I suppose, that we had about decided to hook up with the Kremlin and wanted to discuss matters, so we headed for the only visible door, a big wooden one, standing wide open. We were about twenty paces short of it when somebody inside screamed, a long scream and a real one. A man's scream has more body to it than a woman's. We stopped dead and looked at each other.

The scream came again, longer.

Wolfe jerked his head to the left and moved that way, toward the hole in the wall, on his toes, though it must have killed him. I was right behind. Climbing through the hole would have been a cinch, even for him, if noise hadn't been a factor, but crawling over the rubble silently was complicated. He managed it, and in a moment I was in beside him. We crossed to a door in the inner wall, which was open a crack, probably just as Pasic had left it ten days before, stood to listen, and heard a voice, and then another, from a distance. Then came another scream, a bad one, and while it was still in the air Wolfe opened the door more and stuck his head out. A voice came faintly. Wolfe pulled his head back in and murmured, "They're down below. Let's see."

If there had been a movie camera that would register in that dark corridor, and if I had had it with me, a film of Wolfe trying to navigate that stone floor without making any noise would be something I wouldn't part with. I didn't fully enjoy it at the time, being too busy myself with the problem of moving quietly in the heavy shoes, but it's wonderful to look back at it. At the end was another corridor to the right, narrower and even darker, and ten feet along that took us to the head of a flight of steps going down. The voices were down there. Wolfe started down, going sidewise with his palms flat against the wall, and it was a good thing the steps were stone, since wooden treads would certainly have had something to say to his seventh of a ton. I took the other side right behind him, using the wall too. A thing like that distorts time out of all proportion. It seemed like a good ten minutes on those steps, but afterward I figured it. There were fifteen steps. Say we averaged ten seconds to a step—and it wasn't that much—that would make only two and a half minutes.

At the bottom it was darker still. We turned left, in the direction of the voices, and saw a little spot of light in the

105

left wall twenty feet away. Inching along, we got to it. There was the dim outline of a closed door, and the light was coming through a hole in it, eight inches square, with its center at eye level for a man a little shorter than me. Wolfe started to slide an eye past the edge of the hole, thought better of it, moved an arm's length away from the wall, and looked through the hole. Inside, a man was talking, loud. Wolfe moved closer to the hole, then sidestepped and put his face almost against the door, with his left eye at the right edge of the hole. Taking it as an invitation, I moved beside him and got my right eye at the left edge of the hole. Our ears rubbed.

There were four men in the room. One of them was sitting on a chair with his back to us. Another one was neither sitting nor standing nor laying down. He was hanging. He was over by the far wall, with his arms stretched up and his wrists bound with a cord, and the cord was fastened to a chain suspended from the ceiling. His feet were six inches above the floor. Tied to each ankle was the end of a rope a few feet long, and the other end of each rope was held by a man, one standing off to the right and the other to the left. They were holding the ropes tight enough to keep the subject's feet spread apart a yard or more. The face of the subject was so puffed and contorted that it was half a minute before I realized I had seen him before, and that long again before I placed him. It was Peter Zov, the man with the flat nose, slanting forehead, and low, smooth voice who had been in Gospo Stritar's office, and who had told Wolfe he was a man of action. He was getting action, no question about that, but his voice wouldn't be so low and smooth after the screams he had let loose.

The man in the chair with his back to us, who had been talking, stopped. The two men standing started to pull on the ropes, slow but sure. The gap between the subject's feet widened to four feet, four and a half, five—more, and then no one looking at Peter Zov's face would have recognized him. An inch more, two, and he screamed. I shut my right eye. I must have made some other movement too, for Wolfe gripped my arm. The scream stopped, with a gurgle that was just as bad, and when my eye opened the ropes were slack.

"That won't do, Peter," the man in the chair said. "You are reducing it to a routine. With your keen mind you have calculated that all you have to do is scream, and that time you screamed prematurely. Your scream is not musical,

106

and we may be forced to muffle it. Would you prefer that?"

No answer.

"I repeat," the man in the chair said, "that you are wrong to think you are finished. It is not impossible that we can still find you useful, but not unless you play fair with us. Much of the information you have brought us has been of no account because we already had it. Some of it has been false. You failed completely in the one important operation we have entrusted to you, and your excuses are not acceptable."

"They're not excuses," Peter Zov mumbled. He was choking.

"No? What are they?"

"They're facts. I had to be away."

"You said that before. Perhaps I didn't explain fully enough, so I'll do it more patiently. I am a patient man. I admit that you must make sure to keep your employers convinced that you are to be trusted, since if you don't you are of no value whatever, either to them or to us. I am quite realistic about it. You're being discourteous, Peter; you're not listening to me. Let him down, Bua."

The man on the loft dropped the rope, turned to the wall, unfastened a chain from a peg, and played it out through a pulley on the ceiling. Peter Zov's feet got to the floor, and his arms were lowered, but only until his hands were even with his shoulders. He swayed from side to side as if he were keeping time to slow music.

"That should improve your manners temporarily," the man in the chair told him. "I was saying that I realize you must satisfy that fool, Gospo Stritar, that you serve him well, but you must also satisfy me, which is more difficult because I am not a fool. You could have carried out that operation without the slightest risk of arousing his suspicion, but instead you went to America on a mission for him, and now you have the impudence to come here and expect to be welcomed—even to be paid! So I am paying you. If you answer my questions properly the payment may be more to your taste."

"I had to go," Peter Zov gasped. "I thought you would approve."

"That's a lie. You're not such a blockhead. Those enemies of progress who call themselves the Spirit of the Black Mountain—you know their chief target is the Tito regime, not us, and it suits our purpose for them to make things as difficult as possible for Belgrade. There is little chance.

107

perhaps none, that they will be able to overthrow the regime, but if they do that will suit us even better. We would march in and take over in a matter of hours. Our hostility to the Spirit of the Black Mountain is only a pretense, and you understood that perfectly. The more help they got from America the better. If that lackey of a crook, that Marko Vukcic who made himself rich pandering to the morbid appetites of the bloated American imperialists—if he had increased his help tenfold it would have been a great favor to us. You knew that, and what did you do? At the command of Belgrade you went to America and killed him."

He made a gesture. "If you thought we wouldn't know, you are so big a fool that you would be better dead. The night of March fourth you entered Italy at Gorizia, with papers under the name of Vito Rizzo, and went on to Genoa. You sailed from Genoa as a steward on the *Amilia* on March sixth. She docked at New York on March eighteenth, and you went ashore that night and killed Marko Vukcic and were back on the *Amilia* before nine o'clock. I don't know who briefed you in New York, or whether you had help in such details as stealing the car, but that's of no importance. You stayed aboard the *Amilia* until she sailed on March twenty-first, left her at Genoa on April second, and returned to Titograd that night. I tell you all this so you may know that you can hide nothing from us. Nothing."

He gestured again. "And on Sunday, April fourth, you came here to explain to these men that you had been unable to carry out our operation because you had been sent abroad on a mission. You found a woman here, drinking vodka with them, which was a surprise to you, but a greater surprise was to find that they already knew where you had been and what your mission was. Mistakes were made, I admit it; I only learned of them when I returned to Tirana yesterday from Moscow. They told you that they knew about your mission, and that alarmed you and you fled, and not only that, after you left they told the woman about you. They blame the vodka, but they will learn that it is not a function of vodka to drown a duty. Later they corrected their blunder by disposing of the woman—that is in their favor—but they will have to be taught a lesson."

His tone sharpened. "That can wait, but you can't. Up with him, Bua."

Peter Zov sputtered something, but Bua ignored it. He had it on Peter in bulk, so when he pulled the chain not

108

only Peter's arms went up but also the rest of him. When the feet were well off the floor Bua hooked the chain on the peg and picked up the end of the rope and was ready to resume. So was his colleague.

"Of course," the man in the chair said, "you had to come when you got my message yesterday, since you knew what to expect if you didn't, so that's no credit to you. You can get credit only by earning it. First, once more, how many boats patrol out of Dubrovnik, and what are their schedules?"

"Damn it, I don't know!" Peter was choky again.

"Bah. My patience can't last forever. Split him."

As the men tightened the ropes Wolfe lowered himself to a squat, pulling at my sleeve, and I went down to him. He had the long knife in his right hand. I had been so intent with my eye at the hole that I hadn't seen him take it from his belt. His left hand was fumbling at a pocket. He whispered in my ear, "We're going in when he screams. You open the door, and I go first. Gun in one hand and capsule in the other."

I whispered back, "Me first. No argument. Rescue him?" He nodded. As we straightened up he was still fumbling in his pocket, and I was reaching to the holster for the Marley. It didn't carry the punch of the Colt, but I knew it better. I admit I felt in my pocket to touch the capsule, but I didn't take it out, wanting the hand free. The door should be no problem. On our side was a hasp with a padlock hanging on a chain.

He started to scream. A glance showed me that Wolfe's left hand had left his pocket, and he nodded at me. As I pushed the door open and stepped through, what was at the front of my mind was light. Its source hadn't been visible through the hole. If it was a lamp, as it must be, and if one of them killed it, knives would have it on guns. The only insurance against it would be to plug the three of them in the first three seconds.

I didn't do that, I don't know why—probably because I had never shot a man unless there was nothing else left. The scream drowned the sound of our entry, but Bua saw us and dropped the rope and goggled, and then the other one; and the man in the chair jumped up and whirled to face us. He was closest, and I put the Marley on him. Wolfe, beside me, with the hand that held the knife at his belt level, started to say something but was interrupted. The closest man's hand went for his hip. Either he was a damn fool or a hero, or because I didn't say anything he thought I wasn't serious. I didn't try anything fancy like going for his arm or shoulder, but took him smack in the chest at nine feet. As I moved the gun back to level, the hand of the man on the right darted back and then forward, and how I knew a knife was coming and jerked myself sidewise the Lord only knows. It went by, but he was coming too, pulling something from his belt, and I pressed the trigger and stopped him.

I wheeled left and saw a sight. Bua was at the wall with his knife raised, holding it by the tip, and Wolfe, with his knife still at belt level, was advancing on him step by step, leaning forward in a crouch. When I asked him later why Bua hadn't let fly, he explained elementary knife tactics, saying that you never throw a knife against another knife at less than five meters, because if you don't drop your man in his tracks, which is unlikely if he's in a crouch, you'll be at his mercy. If I had known that I might have tried for Bua's shoulder, but I didn't, and all I wanted was to get a bullet to him before his knife started for Wolfe. I fired, and he leaned against the wall, with his hand still raised. I fired again, and he went down.

This is funny, or call it dumb. Before Bua even hit the floor I turned around to look for the light. I had entered the room with the light on top of my mind, and apparently it had stayed there and I had to get it off. It was a letdown to see that it came from three spots: two lanterns on a shelf to the right of the door, and one on the floor at the left. I had worried about nothing.

Wolfe walked past me to the chair, sat, and said, "Better look at them."

Peter Zov, still hanging, croaked something. Wolfe said, "He wants down. Look at them first. One of them may be shamming."

They weren't. I took my time and made sure. I suspected Bua when I put a piece of fuzz from my jacket on his nostrils, holding his lips shut, and it floated off, but two more tries showed that it had been only a current in the air. "No shamming," I reported. "It was close quarters. If you wanted any—"

"This is what I wanted. Let him down."

I went and took the chain off the peg and eased it up. I suppose I should have been more careful, but my nerves were a little ragged, and when I saw his feet were on the floor I loosened my grip, and his weight jerked the chain out of my hands as he collapsed on the stone. I went to him and got out my pocket knife to cut the cord from his wrists, but Wolfe spoke.

"Wait a minute. Is he alive?"

I inspected him. "Sure he's alive. He just passed out, and I don't blame him."

"Will he die?"

"Of what? Did you bring smelling salts?"

"By heaven," he blurted with sudden ferocity, "you'll clown at your funeral! Tie his ankles and we'll go upstairs. I doubt if the shots could have been heard outside even if there were anyone to hear them, but I want to get out of here."

I obeyed. There was a choice of ropes to tie his ankles with, and it didn't take long. When I finished, Wolfe was at the door with a lantern in his hand, and I got one from the shelf and followed him out and up the fifteen steps. We went up faster than we had come down. He said we had better make sure there was no one else in the fort, and I agreed. He knew his way around as well as if he had built it himself, and we covered it all. He even had me climb the ladder to the tower, while he stood at the foot with my Colt in his hand, talking Albanian—I suppose warning anyone in the tower that if I were attacked he would pump them. When I rejoined him intact we went back to ground level and on outdoors, and he sat down on a flat rock at the corner nearest the trail. On its surface beside him was a big dark blotch.

"That's where Pasic killed the dog," I remarked.

"Yes. Sit down. As you know, I look at people when I talk to them, and I don't like to stretch my neck."

I sat on the blotch. "Oh, you want to talk?"

"I don't want to, I have to. Peter Zov is the man who murdered Marko."

I stared at him. "What is this, a hunch?"

"No. A certainty."

"How come?"

He told me what the man in the chair had said.

XIII

I sat for a minute and chewed on it, squinting at the sun. "If you had told me before we walked in," I said, "it would have taken just one more bullet."

"Pfui. Could you have shot him hanging there?"

"No."

"Then don't try to saddle me with it."

I chewed on it some more. "It's cockeyed. He killed Marko. I killed the birds that killed Carla."

"In a fight. You had no choice. With him we have."

"Name it. You go down and knife him. Or I go and shoot him. Or one of us challenges him to a duel. Or we shove him off a cliff. Or we leave him there to starve." I had an idea. "You wouldn't buy any of those, and neither would I, but what's wrong with this? We turn him over to Danilo and his pals and tell them what you heard. That ought to do it."

"No."

"Okay, it's your turn. We may not have all day because company may come."

"We must take him back to New York."

I guess I gaped. "And you scold me for clowning."

"I'm not clowning. I said with him we have a choice, but we haven't. We are constrained."

"By what?"

"By the obligation that brought us here. What Danilo's wife told him was cogent but not strictly accurate. If personal vengeance were the only factor I could, as you suggested, go and stick a knife in him and finish it, but that would be accepting the intolerable doctrine that man's sole responsibility is to his ego. That was the doctrine of Hitler, as it is now of Malenkov and Tito and Franco and Senator McCarthy; masquerading as a basis of freedom, it is the oldest and toughest of the enemies of freedom. I reject it and condemn it. You look skeptical. I suppose you're thinking that I have sometimes been high-handed in dealing with the hired protectors of freedom in my adopted land—the officers of the law."

"Not more than a thousand times," I protested.

"You exaggerate. But I have never flouted their rightful authority or tried to usurp their lawful powers, and being temporarily in the domain of dictatorial barbarians gives me no warrant to embrace their doctrines and use their methods. Marko was murdered in New York. His murderer is accountable to the People of the State of New York, not to me. Our part is to get him there."

"Hooray for us. The only way to get him there legally is to have him extradited."

"That isn't true. You're careless with your terms. Extradition is the only way to get him there *by action of law,* but that's quite different and of course impossible. The point is to get him under the jurisdiction of civilized law without violating it ourselves."

"I see the point all right. How?"

"That's it. Can he walk?"

"I should think so. I heard no bones crack. Shall I go and find out?"

"No." He got to his feet with only a couple of grunts during the operation. "I must speak with that man—Stan Kosor. I don't want to leave you here alone, because if someone should come you couldn't talk except with the gun, so I'll try this first."

He faced in the direction of Montenegro and beckoned, using the whole length of his arm, again and again. I booked it as a one-to-ten shot, because first, Kosor might not be up in the niche at all, and second, if he was there I doubted if he trusted Wolfe enough to cross the border to him. I lost the bet. I don't know how the man got down from the crag so quickly unless he just let go and slid, but I hadn't even begun to look for him in earnest when my eye was attracted by movement, and there he was on the bend in the trail where it emerged from a defile. He strode along until he reached the spot where the trail began to widen for the space in front of the fort, stopped abruptly, and called something. By then I had seen that it wasn't Kosor but Danilo Vukcic. We had been honored. Wolfe answered him, and he came on.

They jabbered. Danilo sounded and looked as if he didn't believe what he heard, got persuaded apparently, and looked at me with a different expression from any he had had for me before. Deducing that I was being admired for my prowess with small arms, I yawned to show that it was nothing out of the ordinary. Then they got into a hot argument. After that was settled, Wolfe did most of the

113

talking, and there was no more arguing. Evidently everything was rosy, for they shook hands as if they meant it, and Danilo offered me a hand and I took it. He was absolutely cordial. When he went he turned twice, once at the far edge of the wide space and once just before he disappeared into the defile, to wave at us.

"He's a different man," I told Wolfe. "Report, please?"

"There isn't time. I must talk with that man, and we must get away. I told Danilo what happened. He insisted on going down to look at them, but I said no. If he had gone alone he might have come back with a collection of fingers, including Zov's, and if we had gone along and Zov had been conscious he would have seen us together on friendly terms, which wouldn't do. We're going to take Zov out the way we came, and Danilo is going to try to stop us and fail."

"I'm not going to shoot Danilo."

"You won't have to, if he does as agreed, and he will. I would prefer not to go back down there. Will you go? If he can move, bring him here."

"Leave his wrists tied?"

"No. Free him."

I entered the fort by the door, crossed to the entrance to a narrow passage, and after a couple of turns was in the long corridor. At the top of the fifteen steps I turned on my flashlight. Why I got a gun in my hand as I approached the door of the room I don't exactly know, but I did. The lantern on the shelf was still burning. I made the rounds of the three casualties, checked that they still weren't shamming, and then went to Zov. He was stretched out, in a different position from when we left him, with his eyes shut, motionless. I took my knife and cut the rope on his ankles, and then the cord on his wrists, which were red and bruised and swollen, and when I let go of them he tried to let them fall dead to the floor but botched it.

I stood and looked down at him, thinking how much I could simplify matters if I forgot doctrines for just two seconds. Another thought followed it. Was it possible that Wolfe had had that in mind when he sent me down alone, on the chance that I would come back up and report that Zov had kicked off? Let Archie do it? I decided no. I had known him to pull some raw ones, but no.

"Nuts," I told Zov. "Open your eyes."

No sign. I kicked his shoulder, just gently, but the shoulder had had a hard day, and he winced. I stooped and

114

grabbed an ear and started to lift him by it, and his eyes opened and focused on me. I let the ear go, hooked my fingers in his armpits from behind, raised his torso, and hauled him on up. He clutched at my sleeve and said something, and I took hold of his belt in the rear and started him for the door, and he did fine. I was afraid I might have to carry him up the steps, but he made it on his own, though I kept a good hold on the belt for fear he might tumble and break his neck and Wolfe would think I had pushed him. After that there was nothing to it. Halfway down the corridor I shifted from his belt to his elbow, and when we got to the door, in sight of Wolfe, I broke contact. I had some vague feeling that I preferred to have him go on to Wolfe without my touching him. He went to the rock and sat down, and Wolfe moved over a little.

"Well, Mr. Zov," Wolfe said, "I'm glad you can walk."

"Comrade Zov," he said.

"If you like, certainly. Comrade Zov. We'd better be moving. Someone might come, and my son has done enough for one day."

Zov looked at his wrists. It was just as well he didn't have a mirror to look at his face. The flat nose and slanting forehead would never have been a treat, but with the sun on them, and still twitching from spasms, they were something special.

He looked at Wolfe. "You were in Titograd yesterday afternoon. How did you get here?"

"Surely that can wait. We must get away."

"I want to know."

"You heard me mention the Spirit of the Black Mountain. I had been told that one of its leaders could be found here near the border, and we came to find him. We did so, and talked with him, and we were disappointed. We decided to cross into Albania, and saw this fort, and were about to enter, when we heard a scream. We went in to investigate, and you know what we found. We interfered because we disapprove of torture. Violence is often unavoidable, as it was on your mission to New York, but not torture. If that's how—"

"How do you know of my mission to New York?"

"We heard that Russian talking to you. If that's how the Russians do things, we are not their friends. We intend to return to Titograd and see Gospo Stritar. He impressed us." Wolfe stood up without grunting. "Let's go. But did they take anything from you? Weren't you armed?"

"We can't go through the mountains in the daytime. We'll have to hole up—I know a place—until dark."

"No. We're going now."

"That's crazy. We'll never reach the valley alive. It's risky enough at night."

Wolfe tapped him on the shoulder. "It's your nerves, Comrade Zov, and no wonder. But I'm in charge momentarily, and I insist. You have seen my son in action, and you may rely on him to get us through, as I do. I will not undertake that trail again at night, and I refuse to leave you here in your present condition. Were you armed?"

"Yes."

"With a gun?"

"A gun and a knife. They put them in a table drawer." He put his hands on the rock to push himself up. "I'll go get them."

Wolfe halted him with a hand on his shoulder. "You have no energy to waste. My son will go. Alex, a gun and a knife they took from Comrade Zov are in a drawer in a table. Bring them."

"What kind of a gun?"

He asked him and didn't have to relay it. The word "Luger" is neither Serbo-Croat nor Albanian, and I had heard it before. After entering the fort, I went to the first room on the right, which seemed the most likely because I had seen a big table there, and hit it at the first try. At the front of the drawer, with a Luger and a big clasp knife, were a stainless steel wristwatch and a leather fold containing papers, one of them with a red seal and a picture of Peter Zov. He was not photogenic. I went back out with them.

As I approached, Wolfe spoke. "Keep the gun. Give him the knife."

"There's a watch and a fold with papers."

"Give him those." He turned to Zov. "My son will keep the gun for the time being. If an attempt is made to stop us you might be overhasty with it after what you've just gone through."

Zov took the other things and said, "I want the gun."

"You'll get it. Is it an old friend?"

"Yes. I took it from a dead German in the war."

"No wonder you value it. I suppose you had it on your mission to New York."

"I did, and other missions. I want it."

"Later. I assume the responsibility for our safe passage

116

through the mountains, and I don't know you well, though I hope to. You're about my son's age, and it's a pity you can't communicate. Do you know any English at all?"

"I know a few words, like 'okay' and 'dollar' and 'cigarette'."

"I'm sorry I didn't teach him Serbo-Croat. We've been here long enough. I'll lead, and my son will bring up the rear. Come on."

If Zov had had his gun he might have balked, and we would have had either to go on without him or find a place to spend the day. He did try to argue, but Wolfe got emphatic, and I had the gun, so he came. We went to the brook for a drink and then hit the trail, with Zov in between us. His gait was more of a shuffle than a walk, but he didn't seem to be in any great pain. It could have been as much from lack of enthusiasm as from the condition of his legs. When we had passed through the defile and topped a rise, and Wolfe stopped for breath, I asked him, "Where will the charade be? You didn't tell me."

"It isn't necessary. We'll keep colloquy at a minimum. Statements about linguistic proficiency may be equivocal. I'll tell you when to draw a gun."

"You might tell me now about the colloquy you just had."

He did so, and then turned and proceeded. As I padded along behind I was thinking that we certainly had the bacon—not only the murderer but the weapon, and I knew the rest of the evidence was on file because I had seen the assistant medical examiner getting it from Marko's corpse. I remembered the first sentences of a book I had read on criminology. *In criminal investigations,* it said, *the investigator must always have in mind the simple basic requirements. Once he gains possession of the person of the criminal and of evidence adequate for conviction, the job is done.* It is, like hell, I thought. If I had that book here, and the author, I'd make him eat it.

I was supposed to forget about being stopped and leave it to Wolfe, but as we approached the point where one left the trail if one was ass enough to want to walk the ledge to the cave, I kept close behind Zov and had my eyes peeled. We went on by without sight or sound of anyone. If you wonder why Wolfe didn't let me know, which he could have done in ten words, I can tell you. I would have had to put on an act for Zov's benefit until I reached the spot that had been agreed on, and he thought I might overdo it or

117

underdo it, I don't know which. He thought that, not knowing, I would just act natural. You may also wonder why I didn't resent it. I did. I had been resenting it for years, but that was my first crack at resenting it in the mountains of Montenegro.

With the sun nearly straight above us, blazing down, I wouldn't have recognized the trail as the one we had climbed the night before with Danilo. We went down rock faces on our rumps, skirted the edges of cliffs, slithered down stretches of loose shale, and at one place crossed a crevice ten feet wide, on a narrow plank bridge with no rails, which I didn't remember at all. My watch said ten minutes past one when we stopped at a brook for a drink and a meal of chocolate. Comrade Zov ate as much chocolate as Wolfe and me together.

Half an hour later the trail suddenly spilled us out at the edge of a wide level space, and there was the house Wolfe had been born in. I stopped for a look. Apparently its back wall was the side of a cliff. It had two stories, with a roof that sloped four ways from the center, and eight windows on the side I was looking at, four below and four above. The glass in three windows was broken. The door was wooden.

I was just starting to turn to tell Wolfe I was going to step inside for a glance around when his voice snapped at my back, "Gun, Alex!"

I whirled, drawing the Colt from my hip. Danilo, Josip Pasic, and two other men were grouped at the far edge of the space, evidently having come from behind a massive boulder. Danilo had a gun, but the others were empty-handed.

"Don't shoot," Danilo said. "You can go wherever you're going. We only want Peter Zov."

Wolfe had put himself in front of Zov. "He's with us, and he's going with us."

"No, he's not. We're taking him."

Wolfe's attitude was perfect for saying "Over my dead body," but he didn't say it. My own attitude was no slouch, with my feet planted apart and my Colt steady at Danilo's belly. Wolfe said, "He's under our protection, and you can't have him. We're American citizens, and if you harm us you'll regret it."

"We don't want to harm you. Zov is a traitor to his country. He crossed the border to the Albanians. We have a right to him."

"What do you intend to do with him?"

"I'm going to find out what he told the Albanians."

They must have been ad libbing, for there hadn't been time to write a script during their brief talk at the fort.

"I don't believe it," Wolfe said. "After the hours I spent with you, I don't believe anything you say. Heaven only knows where your allegiance lies, if anywhere. If you are a true son of Yugoslavia, come with us—you alone, not the others. If Zov has betrayed his country the proper person to deal with him is Gospo Stritar in Titograd, and that's where we're taking him. If you want to come, drop your gun and start down the road. You others stay where you are."

"We'll deal with him here."

"You will not. Are you coming?"

"No."

"Then touch us at your peril. Comrade Zov, I'm going to turn around. You turn also, to face the road entrance. Keep against me, away from them, and we'll make the road slowly, and on down. Alex, cover us. You'll have to back out, steering by my voice."

He turned and had his back to the enemy. Zov turned likewise, and Wolfe put his hands on Zov's shoulders. I sidestepped and was directly behind Wolfe, back to back, with the Colt still focused on the group. As Wolfe and Zov moved forward, and I backward, Wolfe gave me his voice to guide by.

" 'Preamble. We, the People of the United States, in order to form a more perfect Union, establish justice, insure domestic tranquility, provide for the common defense, promote the general welfare, and secure the blessings of liberty to ourselves and our posterity, do ordain and establish this Constitution for the United States of America.' "

We had left the open space and started down the road. Since Zov couldn't possibly see me, I had a strong impulse to grin at Danilo and to wave to him as he had waved to us when he left the fort. I had to bite my lip to control it. He might misunderstand and ruin everything.

Wolfe was guiding me. "I skip to the ten original amendments, the Bill of Rights. 'Article One. Congress shall make no law respecting an establishment of religion, or prohibiting the free exercise thereof; or abridging the freedom of speech or of the press; or the right of the people peaceably to assemble and to petition the Government for a redress of grievances. Article Two. A well-regulated militia being necessary to the security of a free State, the right of the people to keep and bear arms shall not be infringed. Article Three. No soldier shall, in time of peace, be quartered in any house without the consent of the owner, nor in time of war but in a manner to be prescribed by law. Article Four. The right—' "

"Hold it," I cut in. "I'm not going to back clear to Titograd."

"I'll finish Article Four. It's Article Four that has us in this mess. 'The right of the people to be secure in their persons, houses, papers, and effects, against unreasonable searches and seizures, shall not be violated, and no warrants shall issue but upon probable cause, supported by oath or affirmation, and particularly describing the place to be searched, and the persons or things to be seized.' "

"Is that all?"

"That will do."

I turned around.

XIV

We arrived in Titograd in style, in an old Ford truck that Zov requisitioned at the first farm we came to that had one, and pulled up in front of police headquarters at twenty minutes past three, just twenty-two hours after Jubé Bilic had delivered us there the day before. As we piled out, Wolfe told me to give the driver three thousand dinars, and I obeyed. I was stuck again with the knapsacks, which we had taken off when we boarded the truck, and with the sweaters. We followed Zov into the big old stone edifice, along the dingy corridor, up the stairs, and into the room where the two clerks sat on stools. Zov spoke to Wolfe, and Wolfe told me we were to wait there and went to a chair and sat. Zov didn't go on in. He sent one of the clerks, who entered the inner room, returned in a moment, and motioned Zov to come. I put the luggage on a chair beside Wolfe and myself on another one.

It was a long wait, so long that I began to nurse the possibility that Gospo Stritar was going to relieve us of our problem. Evidently Zov had been completely confident that his loyalty would not be questioned, but Stritar might not see it that way. The idea had its attractions, but it led to another, that if a visit to the Albanians was enough to do for Zov, what about Toné Stara and his son Alex? That wasn't so attractive. I would have liked to ask Wolfe a couple of pertinent questions, but his head had fallen forward until his chin touched, his eyes were closed, and he was breathing as if he were a week behind on oxygen, so I let him alone.

I became aware that someone was yelling at somebody named Alex, and wished Alex would answer. Also someone had hold of my shoulder. I opened my eyes, saw Wolfe, and jerked upright.

"You were sound asleep," he said testily.

"So were you. First."

"We're wanted. Bring the knapsacks."

I gathered them up and followed him between the counters and across to the inner room. Zov, holding the door for us, shut it and went to a chair at the end of Stritar's desk and sat. Stritar waved us to chairs without getting up. He hadn't got a haircut. His underhung jaw didn't seem quite as impressive as it had the day before, but I had seen a lot of underhung rocks in the meantime. After giving Wolfe a sharp glance, he concentrated on me as I went to the chair, and after I sat he looked me up and down. Not knowing what our line was going to be, or his either, I neither grinned nor glowered at him but merely looked self-reliant.

He turned to Wolfe. "It's too bad your son doesn't speak our language. I'd like to talk with him."

Wolfe nodded. "I was wrong not to teach him. I would be glad to interpret for you."

"That's not the same. Comrade Zov has told me what happened today. You and your son have acted boldly and bravely. It is appreciated by me and will be appreciated by my superiors. You can add to that appreciation by giving me a full account of your movements since you left here yesterday."

Wolfe raised his brows. "I'm surprised that you ask. You said everything would get to you."

"Perhaps it has. I would like to hear it from you."

"You may. We went first to the house where I visited my friend Grudo Balar many years ago. A stranger was there who had never heard of him. We went next to an address that someone in Albania had given me. I had been

121

told that a man named Danilo Vukcic could give me much information if he would, particularly about the Spirit of the Black Mountain."

"Who in Albania told you about him?"

Wolfe shook his head. "I told you yesterday that I will not cause trouble for anyone who has helped us. We found Danilo Vukcic at that address, and he did indeed have information. It seemed to me that he was overready to impart it to strangers, but later, thinking it over, I realized that it was only such matters as were probably common knowledge—or merely current rumors. I was quite candid with him. You may remember I told you that we had cached a considerable sum in American dollars somewhere in the mountains, and I told him about it too. I now think that was a mistake. I now think it was my telling him about that cache that caused him to offer to take us to a place in the mountains where we could meet one of the leaders of the Spirit of the Black Mountain. Anyway, we accepted the offer, and he took us. After a difficult journey we arrived—"

"One moment. Did you see Jubé Bilic anywhere? The boy who brought you here yesterday?"

Wolfe was surprised and puzzled. "Him? Where? In the mountains?"

"Did you see him anywhere after you left here?"

"I did not. Why?"

Stritar waved it away. "Go on."

"We arrived at a cave—near the Albanian border, I was told—in the middle of the night. There were five men there, and Vukcic said that one of them was a leader of the Spirit, but he didn't impress me as a leader of men or of a movement. By that—"

"What was his name?"

"I was given no names. By that time I was suspicious of the whole business. They insisted on knowing where our dollars were cached, and at one time I thought they were going to try to force us to tell by methods that I consider barbarous. Also I distrusted Vukcic. I have had many dealings with men, mostly in America, and I concluded that Vukcic was not honest or sincere, and that I would have nothing to do with a movement in which he was prominent or influential. I didn't tell him that, of course. If I had we might not have left the mountains alive, in spite of the fact that they would rather not lay a hand on American citizens. The question was, how to get away from them without serious trouble, and I think I managed it pretty well. In the morning I said we would like to have a look at the border, at Albania, and Vukcic went with us to show us where the border is, since it isn't marked. When we got there we simply kept on going. Vukcic wanted to stop us, but we paid no attention to him. He stuck to us for a distance, protesting, but stopped when we emerged from a defile. We soon knew why, when we saw the fort. We went to it and were about to enter, when we heard a scream, and we went in to investigate. You have heard the rest from Comrade Zov."

"I want to hear it from you. All of it—if you can, every word."

When Wolfe reported to me later, I liked that. Up to that point the indications were that Stritar really trusted Zov, which would have been silly. The one rule everybody in Yugoslavia stuck to was: never trust anybody, anywhere, any time.

I don't need to report the rest of it to you, as Wolfe didn't to me. He gave it to Stritar just as it had happened, omitting only his conversations with me and Danilo's visit to the fort. I will, however, include something that he tacked on at the end, after he had got us into the truck on our way to Titograd. "My son and I," he said, "claim no special credit for what we did, but you expressed appreciation for it. If you would like us to have a token of your appreciation, one little favor would be welcome. For some time my son has wanted a Luger pistol, and he says that Comrade Zov's is in excellent condition. He would like to trade his Colt for it if Comrade Zov is willing."

Of course I didn't know then what he had said, but I saw he had made a mistake. Zov's reaction, which was prompt, was merely a loud and emphatic protest, but Stritar narrowed his eyes and tightened his lips. Later, when I learned what Wolfe had said, I thanked God Stritar hadn't been quite keen enough. He had suspected there was something phony about it, but he hadn't gone a step further and realized that Toné Stara was from America and that Zov's gun had been used to commit a murder in America. If he had, good-by. I'm not blaming Wolfe for making the try. He wanted me to hang on to that Luger if I possibly could, and he took the chance. He saw at once that it wouldn't work and he had nearly gummed it, and was quick to repair the damage.

He raised a hand to stop Zov's protest. "No, Comrade

Zov, not if you feel so strongly about it. It was just a suggestion, of no importance. I thought you might welcome it. Alex, give Comrade Zov his gun."

I took it from my pocket, went over and handed it to him, and returned to my chair.

Stritar's eyes were back to normal. "You will be glad to know that your account agrees in every respect with Peter Zov's. Of course you could have arranged for that, there was plenty of time, but I have at present no reason to suppose that you did. You can tell your son that the man he killed was Dmitri Shuvalov, one of the three top Russians in Albania."

Wolfe told me, and I said that was interesting.

"So," Stritar said, "I'm glad I let you go yesterday, to see what you would get into. I certainly didn't anticipate your performance at the fort. Zov, who speaks Russian, has been in contact with Shuvalov for some time, and was doing well, he thought; but evidently he was wrong. It was lucky for him you came along, and I tell you frankly, you have earned some consideration. What are you going to do now? Would you like to go to Belgrade? It is not out of the question for you to meet the marshal."

"We have no papers, as you know."

"That will be no difficulty, under the circumstances."

"I don't know." Wolfe looked doubtful. "My son and I feel that we have accomplished what we came for. It doesn't take us a year to tell an apple from a wart. We are satisfied that the true interests of the people of my native land will be best served by the present regime. We were particularly impressed by your treatment of us yesterday, because it could only have come from the confidence of a secure and just authority. We want to help as far as our modest resources will permit, but we can do more good in America than we could here. Our property is there, and our—oh, by the way, speaking of property, I told you of our cache in the mountains."

"Yes."

"It's eight thousand dollars in American currency, and we wish to contribute it as a token of our belief in the regime and our desire to support it. I'll tell my son what I have said so he may indicate his concurrence." He turned to me. "Alex, I'm telling them that we donate our cache of eight thousand dollars to the regime. If you agree, please nod at them."

I did so, first at Stritar and then at Zov. But if I know

124

anything about men's faces, having seen the look they exchanged as Wolfe spoke, all the regime would ever see of that eight grand wouldn't get the windows washed in that one room. I took in their expressions as Wolfe proceeded to furnish in careful detail the location of the cache, and I'll bet I had them right. Zov was thinking: It ought to be an even split. I brought them here. Stritar was thinking: Ten per cent is enough for Zov. He's lucky to be in on it at all.

Wolfe went on, "Of course that amount is nothing, it's merely a gesture, but we wish to make it. When we get back to America we'll see what we can do. You suggested our going to Belgrade, but that doesn't appeal to us. Our interest centers in the people of these mountains, and even under the present progressive regime they seem to be a little neglected. Also I like to deal with men I have met, men I know. From America I would rather be in touch with you than with names in Belgrade that mean nothing to me personally. I suppose you regard that as a bourgeois sentiment."

"Well." Stritar considered it. "It's human."

Wolfe looked apologetic. "I admit I have acquired some bourgeois habits of thought during my years in America, and that is regrettable. I am of peasant origin. The peasant is out of date, and the bourgeois is doomed. You and your kind represent the future, and my son wants to be a part of the future. I intend to teach him Serbo-Croat, and in time, when our affairs in America have been properly arranged, he hopes to return here for good. Meanwhile I shall communicate with you, and you can tell me now if you have any suggestions how we can be of use."

"We need friends in America," Stritar said.

"Naturally. You need friends everywhere. We will do what we can in that direction. Would you advise us to join the Communist Party of the United States and try to influence them in your favor?"

"Good God, no." Stritar was contemptuous. "They belong to Moscow, body and soul, and they're a nest of slimy vermin. Where do you live in America?"

"In Philadelphia."

"Where is that?"

"It's a city with two million people, ninety miles southwest of New York."

"Two million! That's incredible. Is your name there Toné Stara?"

"No." Wolfe hesitated. "It is not a question of being frank with you, Comrade Stritar. It is merely that I would not want any inquiries made among my friends or associates until I return. As soon as I arrive I'll let you know, and of course give you my American name and address. One thing you should tell me now; in case I have money to send, which is very probable, I would want to be sure it reaches you safely. How would I send dollars?"

Stritar pursed his lips. "I'll think it over and let you know. You're right, it should be properly arranged. When are you leaving, and how?"

"We have no papers."

"I know."

"Also, I'll be frank, we want to get away as soon ⸱ possible. You must forgive us if we feel that we are in danger. I know that the police here are under you and are therefore extremely efficient, but today we heard that Russian tell Comrade Zov that he had to come to the fort when he got his message, because he knew what to expect if he didn't. So not only can they get messages to Titograd, but also if the messages are not heeded they can do something about it. They will certainly not let the death of that Dmitri Shuvalov go unavenged, not to mention the other two. We are not comfortable in Titograd."

"No one saw you. No one knows you were there."

"Danilo Vukcic knows, and his friends. My suspicions of Vukcic may be unfounded, but I have them. He may be in Albania now, to report about us. And that suggests another matter, though it is not our concern."

"What other matter?"

Wolfe glanced at Zov and back at Stritar. "Regarding Comrade Zov. I presume his danger is greater than ours. If Shuvalov was confident that he could reach him in Titograd to punish him for ignoring a message, surely they can reach him when the motive is so much stronger. That is his concern, and yours, but, having rescued him from torture and perhaps death, naturally we feel an interest in him. I am willing to propose something if it is not impertinent."

"You couldn't be more impertinent than to march into my office and announce you had no papers. What do you propose?"

"That you send Zov to America for a while. He could either go with us or come to us after he arrives, and we would see to his needs and his safety. It offers several advantages: it would remove him temporarily from peril here,

126

if there is any; it would give us someone in America who is familiar with conditions here, to advise us; it would give you an agent there whom you trust, to report on us and our associates; and it would give me a messenger I could rely on if I had something confidential or valuable to send to you." Wolfe flipped a hand. "Of course, for some reason unknown to me, it may be quite impractical."

Stritar and Zov had exchanged not one glance, but several. Stritar said, "It is worth considering. It may not be entirely impractical."

"I thought it might not be," Wolfe said, "since Zov returned only recently from a trip to America. That was what suggested it to me. I even thought it possible you might have another mission for him there. If so, he might need help, and what we did today, especially my son, may have demonstrated that we could be capable of supplying it."

Stritar looked at Zov. Then he studied Wolfe. Then he transferred to me. I was aware, from tones and expressions and the atmosphere, that we were at a crisis, but I didn't know what kind, so all I could do was meet his eyes and look loyal and confident and absolutely intrepid. After he had analyzed me clear through to my spine he returned to Wolfe.

"Did you ever," he asked, "hear of a man named Nero Wolfe?"

I claim a medal for handling not only my face but all my nerves and muscles. His pronunciation was fuzzy, but not too fuzzy for me to get it. I knew they were at a crisis, and suddenly that bozo snaps out the name Nero Wolfe. How I kept my hand from starting for my holster I don't know. Wolfe showed no sign of panic, but that was no help. He wouldn't panic if you paid him.

"Of course," he said. "If you mean the well-known detective in New York. Everyone in America has heard of him."

"Do you know him?"

"I haven't met him, no. I know a man who has. He says I look like him, but I've seen a picture of him, and the only resemblance is that we're both big and fat."

"Did you know a man named Marko Vukcic?"

"No, but I heard his name today, as I told you, when Shuvalov was speaking to Zov. Was he any relation to Danilo Vukcic?"

"His uncle. He owned a de luxe restaurant. This detective, Nero Wolfe, was his friend, and there is reason to believe that he intends to take Vukcic's place and send money and other help to the Spirit of the Black Mountain. In large amounts."

Wolfe grunted. "Then it did no good to kill Vukcic."

"I don't agree. We couldn't know that a friend of his would take over so promptly and effectively. But he has. I got the news only today."

"And now you propose to kill Nero Wolfe."

Stritar snapped, "I didn't say so."

"No, but you might as well. I haven't got a quick mind, but it didn't have to be quick for that. I suggested that you might have another mission for Zov in America, and you asked me if I had ever heard of this Nero Wolfe. That's just adding two and two, or rather one and one. So you propose to kill him."

"What if I do?"

"It may be necessary. I don't know."

"You told Zov that you disapprove of torture but that violence is often unavoidable, as it was on his mission to New York."

"That's true. I meant that. But I don't think a man should be killed merely on suspicion. Have you any evidence that this Nero Wolfe will really help your enemies as Vukcic did?"

"I have." Stritar opened a drawer of his desk and took out a paper. "Day before yesterday a man in Bari received a telegram from Nero Wolfe which read as follows: 'Inform proper persons across Adriatic I am handling Vukcic's affairs and assuming obligations. Two hundred thousand dollars available soon. Will send agent conference Bari next month.'" Stritar put the paper back and shut the drawer. "Is that evidence?"

"It sounds like it. Who is the man in Bari that got the telegram?"

"That's not important. You want to know too much."

"I don't think so, Comrade Stritar—if I am to call you Comrade. If I am to trust you on vital matters, as I am prepared to do, you will trust me to some extent. My son and I will have to go through Bari on our way back, to get our papers and effects, and we might possibly encounter him. His name?"

Stritar shrugged his bulging shoulders. "Paolo Telesio."

Wolfe's eyes widened. "What!"

Stritar stared. "What's the matter?"

"Enough." Wolfe was grim. "Paolo Telesio has our pa-

128

pers and belongings. We left them in his care. A man in Philadelphia gave me his name, as one trustworthy and capable, who would arrange for getting us across the Adriatic. And he serves the Spirit of the Black— No, wait! After all, you have that telegram." He shook his head. "No, it is just as well we're going back. Here it's impossible to tell who you're dealing with. My brain is not equipped for it."

"Not many brains are," Stritar declared. "Don't make any assumptions about Telesio. I didn't say he sent me the telegram. You are not to tell him I have seen it. You understand that?"

"Certainly. We're not a pair of fools, though yesterday you called us that. Do you still think so?"

"I think it is possible I was wrong. I agree with you that you can do more good in America than you can here. It is in your favor that you are inclined to be skeptical, as for instance about Nero Wolfe. You asked for evidence that he intends to send major assistance to our subversive underground, and I furnished it. I regard it as conclusive. Do you?"

Wolfe hesitated. "Conclusive is a strong word. But I— yes. I will say yes."

"Then he must be dealt with. Will you help?"

"That depends. If you mean will I or my son engage to kill him, no. Killing a man in America is not the same as killing a man here. Circumstances might develop that would lead us to undertake it, but I won't commit myself, and neither will he."

"I didn't ask you to. I asked if you'll help. Peter Zov will need it. The preparations and arrangements will have to be made for him, and provision for his safety afterward. You say Philadelphia is ninety miles from New York—that's a hundred and fifty kilometers—and that is well, for New York would be dangerous for him. That's the kind of help he'll need. Will you give it?"

Wolfe considered. "There's a difficulty. No matter how well it is arranged, it's conceivable that Zov will be caught. If he is, under pressure he might betray us."

"You saw him under pressure today. Will the American police use greater pressure than that?"

"No." Wolfe looked at me. "Alex, it is suggested that Comrade Zov shall go to America, and we shall provide for his necessities and also help him with the preparations to kill a man named Nero Wolfe. I am willing to undertake it if you are."

I looked serious. I would have given eight thousand cents to be able to reply that I had been wanting to kill a man named Nero Wolfe for years, but I wasn't sure that Stritar and Zov understood no English. I had to skip it. I said earnestly, "I am willing, Father, to help with anything you approve of."

He looked at Stritar. "My son says he is willing. We want to leave here as soon as possible. Can you get us to Bari tonight?"

"Yes. But Zov will have to go by another route." Stritar looked at his watch. "There is much to arrange." He raised his voice to call, "Jin!"

The door opened, and one of the clerks came in. Stritar spoke to him. "Find Trumbic and Levstik and get them here. I'll be busy for an hour or more. No interruptions unless it's urgent."

Zov had his Luger out, rubbing it with his palm.

XV

We got arrested for having no papers after all, and it damn near bollixed everything.

Not in Montenegro. Stritar took no chances on our changing our minds and deciding to go to Belgrade, where we would probably mention the eight thousand dollars and the promise of more to come. He fed us there in his office, on meat and cheese and bread and raisins that he had brought in, and a little after dark took us down to the street himself and put us in a 1953 Ford, a different color from Jubé Bilic's. Our destination was Budva, a coast village which Wolfe said was five miles north of the spot where we had been landed by Guido Battista two nights before. During the hour and a half that it took to cover the thirty miles, the driver had no more than a dozen words for Wolfe, and none at all for me. As he delivered us at the edge of a slip and exchanged noises with a man waiting there, it started to rain.

It rained all the way across the Adriatic, but the boat was a few centuries newer than Guido's, with a cabin where I could lie down. Wolfe tried it too, but the bench was so narrow he had to grip a bracket to keep from rolling off, and finally he gave up and stretched out on the floor. The boat, with a crew of two besides the skipper, was fast, noisy, was rated 500 v.p.m., which means vibrations per minute, and was a steeplechaser. It loved to jump waves. No wonder it beat Guido's time by nearly three hours. It was still raining, and dark as pitch, when it anchored in choppy water and we were herded into a dinghy some bigger than Guido's. The skipper rowed us into the wall of night until he hit bottom, dumped us on the beach, shoved the nose of the dinghy off, hopped in, and was gone.

Wolfe called to him, "Confound it, where are we?"

He called back, "Where you're supposed to be!"

"The genial sonofabitch," I remarked.

With the sweaters draped over our heads, and flashlights, we headed inland. A road going to Molfetta, a fishing village two miles away if we had been landed in the right place, was supposed to be only two hundred yards from the shore, and we found it, turned left, and trudged along in the rain. It was 3:28 a.m. when we hit the road. I was thinking that when we got to the stucco house in Bari I would have Wolfe translate the directions on the water heater in the bathroom.

We made it to Molfetta, knocked at the door of a white house with trees in front, and Wolfe spoke through a crack to the man who unlocked it, and handed him a slip of paper. He was about as genial as the skipper had been, but he agreed to drive us to Bari, twenty five kilometers down the coast, for five thousand lire. We weren't invited in out of the rain. We waited under a tree, a European species called a dripping tree, while he put on some clothes, and when he appeared on the driveway in a little Fiat we climbed in the back and sat on wet fannies and were off.

I took my mind off the wet by thinking. Wolfe had reported in full on the boat. There were some aspects that seemed to me a little sour, such as donating the eight grand to that character, but I had to admit he was justified in making his proposal as tempting to Stritar as he possibly could. The only bad flaw was that we didn't have Zov, and no guarantee that we would get him again. He was to sneak into Italy at Gorizia, as he had before, I don't know how often, and meet us at Genoa. Wolfe explained that even if Stritar had been willing to send him with us through Bari, having him along would have made matters very difficult.

I was going over it when suddenly the car stopped, the left front door opened, and a beam of light focused on the driver. A man in a raincoat was there. He asked the driver some questions and got answered, and then opened the rear door, aimed the light at us, and spoke. Wolfe replied. It developed into quite a chat, with the man insisting on something and Wolfe insisting back. Finally the man shut the door, circled around the hood to the right front door, got in beside the driver, spoke to him, and twisted in the seat to face us. His hand, resting on the back of the seat, had a gun in it.

I asked Wolfe, "Am I supposed to do something?"

"No. He wanted to see our papers."

"Where are we going?"

"Jail."

"But my God, aren't we in Bari?"

"Entering it, yes."

"Then tell him to take us to that house and we'll show him the damn papers."

"No. At the risk of having it get across the Adriatic tomorrow that I am here? Impossible."

"What did you tell him?"

"That I wish to see the American consul. Naturally he refuses to disturb him at this hour."

I am thinking of starting a movement to push for a law requiring two consuls in every city, a day consul and a night consul, and you would join it if you had ever spent a night, or part of one, in the hoosegow at Bari. We were questioned—or Wolfe was—first by a handsome baritone in a slick unifrom and then by a fat animal in a soiled seersucker. Our guns and knives didn't make them any more cordial. Then we were locked in a cell with two cots which were already occupied by fifty thousand others. Twenty thousand of the others were fleas, and another twenty thousand were bedbugs, but I never found out what the other ten thousand were. After a night in a haystack and one in a deep-freeze cave, it would have been reasonable to suppose that anything different would be an improvement, but it wasn't. I got a lot of walking done, back and forth the full length of the cell, a good ten feet, being careful not to step on Wolfe, who was sitting on the concrete floor. All I will say about the breakfast is that we didn't eat it. The chocolate, what was left of it, was in the knapsacks, and they had been taken.

Another section of that law will provide that day consuls will get to work at eight o'clock. It was after ten when the door of the cell opened and a man appeared and said something. Wolfe told me to come, and we were conducted down a corridor and some stairs and into a sunny room where two men sat talking. One of them spoke; and then the other, a lanky, tired-looking specimen with ears as big as saucers, said in American, "I'm Thomas Arnold, the American consul. I'm told you want to see me."

"I have to see you"—Wolfe glanced at the other man—"in private."

"This is Signor Angelo Bizzaro, the warden."

"Thank you. All the same, privacy is essential. We are not armed."

"I'm told that you were." Arnold turned and spoke to the warden, and after a little exchange Bizzaro got up and left the room. "Now what is it?" Arnold demanded. "Are you American citizens?"

"We are. The quickest way to dispose of this, Mr. Arnold, would be for you to telephone the embassy in Rome and ask for Mr. Richard Courtney."

"Not until you tell me who you are and why you were out on the road at night, armed, with no papers."

"You'll have to know who we are, of course," Wolfe agreed. "And so will the police, but I hope through you to arrange that our presence here will not be published. I thought a talk with Mr. Courtney would help, but it's not essential. My name is Nero Wolfe. I am a licensed private detective with an office in New York. This is my assistant, Archie Goodwin."

The consul was smiling. "I don't believe it."

"Then telephone Mr. Courtney. Or, perhaps better, do you know a man in Bari, a broker and agent, named Paolo Telesio?"

"Yes. I've met him."

"If you'll phone him and let me speak to him, he'll bring our passports, properly stamped at Rome when we arrived there on Sunday, four days ago. Also he'll identify us."

"I'll be damned. You *are* Nero Wolfe?"

"I am."

"Why the hell were you wandering around at night with guns and knives and no papers?"

"That was indiscreet but necessary. We are here on an important and confidential matter, and our presence must not be known."

I thought he was doing fine. His asking Arnold to phone the embassy would make the consul suspect that we were on a secret job for the State Department, and if he phoned and Courtney told him we weren't that would only make him think the job was supersecret. He didn't get the embassy, at least not from there. He got Telesio, let Wolfe talk to him, and then sat and chewed the fat with us until Telesio arrived with the passports. Wolfe had pressed it on him that as few people as possible should know we were there, so he didn't tell even the warden our names. He made another phone call, and another signor came, who looked and acted more important than a warden, and he looked at our passports and made it legal for us to breathe. When we left with Telesio they shook hands with us, perfectly friendly, but I noticed they avoided any close contact, which was understandable. They knew where we had been for five hours, that we hadn't been alone, and that some of our companions were leaving with us.

Telesio knew it too. When he stopped the car in the courtyard of the stuccoed house, and we got out and followed the path to the door, he spoke to Wolfe and Wolfe turned to me. "We'll undress in the hall and throw these things outdoors."

We did so. Telesio brought a chair for Wolfe, but I said I didn't need one. Our first donning of those duds was in that house, and so was our first doffing. I won't go into detail except for Wolfe's shoes and socks. He was afraid to take them off. When he finally set his jaw and pitched in, he gazed at his feet in astonishment. I think he had expected to see nothing but a shapeless mass of raw red flesh, and it wasn't bad at all, only a couple of heel blisters and a rosy glow, and the toes ridged and twisted some.

"They'll be back to normal in a year easy," I told him. I didn't have to ask him for help with the water heater because Telesio had already gone up and turned it on.

Two hours later, at a quarter past one, we were in the kitchen with Telesio, eating mushroom soup and spaghetti and cheese, and drinking wine, clean and dressed and sleepy. Wolfe had phoned to Rome and had an appointment with Richard Courtney at the embassy at five o'clock. Telesio had arranged for a plane to be ready for us at the Bari airport at two-thirty. I never asked Wolfe for a full report of his conversation with Telesio that day, and probably wouldn't have got it if I had, but I did want to know about two points, and he told me. First, what did Telesio think of letting Stritar cop the eight grand? He had thought it was unnecessary, immoral, and outrageous. Second, what did Telesio think of what Wolfe had said to Stritar about

Danilo Vukcic? Did he agree with me that Wolfe may have put Danilo on a spot? No. He said Danilo was a very smooth customer, and for three years Stritar had been trying to decide whether he was coming or going, and in what direction, and nothing Wolfe had said would hurt him any. That relieved my mind. I had hated to think that we might have helped to reprive Meta of her provider of flour to make bread with. I was telling Fritz only yesterday he should go to a certain address in Titograd and learn how to make bread.

There had been a three-way argument in two languages, which made it complicated. Wolfe's initials were not on his bag, but they were on his made-to-order shirts and pajamas. How much of a risk was there that Zov would snoop around and see them, and get suspicious, and also maybe get a bright idea? Wolfe thought it was slight, but we ganged up on him and he gave in. The shirts and pajamas were left behind, to be shipped by Telesio, and Telesio went out and bought replacements, which were pretty classy but not big enough. My bag had my initials on it, but we agreed that AG wasn't as risky as NW—that is, they agreed, and I said I did, not caring to start another argument.

Telesio drove us to the airport in the Fiat, which still didn't have a dent, though he hadn't changed his attitude on obstructions. There were more people and activity at the airport than there had been on Palm Sunday, but apparently word had been passed along by the signor who had legalized us, for Telesio merely popped into a room with our passports and popped right out again, and took us out to a plane that was waiting on the apron. With tears in his eyes—which didn't mean he was suffering, because I had noticed that they came when he laughed—he kissed Wolfe on both cheeks and me on one, and stood and watched us take off.

Since on our way in we hadn't left the airport, I couldn't say I had been in Rome, but now I can. A taxi took us through the city to the American embassy, and later another one took us back to the airport, so I know Rome like a book. It has a population of 1,695,477, and has many fine old buildings.

When we entered one of the buildings, the embassy, we were ten minutes early for our appointment, but we didn't have to wait. A young woman who was fair enough at the moment but would have two chins in a few years if she

135

didn't take steps was obviously interested in us, which was natural, since Wolfe declined to give our names, saying only that we were expected by Mr. Courtney; and she had been briefed, for after a quick survey trying to guess whether we were CIA or just a couple of congressmen trying to be cagey, she used a phone, and before long Richard Courtney appeared, greeted us diplomatically without pronouncing names, and escorted us within, to a little room halfway down a long, wide corridor. Three chairs were about all it had room for without crowding. He invited us to take two of them and went to the third, which was behind a desk stacked with papers.

He eyed us. Superficially he was still a distinguished-looking college boy, but a lot more reserved than four days earlier. From the way he looked at us, he wasn't exactly suspicious, but he intended to find out whether he ought to be.

"You said on the phone," he told Wolfe, "that you wanted to ask a favor."

"Two favors," Wolfe corrected him. "One was to let us get to you without mention of names."

"That has been done. I've mentioned your name, since you phoned, only to Mr. Teague, the Secretary. What's the other one?"

"I'll make it as brief as possible. Mr. Goodwin and I came to Italy on an important and confidential matter, a private matter. During our stay on Italian soil we have violated no law and committed no offense, except the minor one of being abroad without our papers. Our errand is satisfactorily completed and we're ready to go home, but there is a small difficulty. We wish to sail tomorrow from Genoa on the *Basilia,* but incognito. The success of our errand will be compromised if it is known that we are sailing on the ship. From Bari I telephoned the Rome office of the steamship company and was able to reserve a double cabin in the names of Carl Gunther and Alex Gunther. I want to go there now and get the tickets. I ask you to telephone them and tell them it's all right to let me have them."

"You mean to guarantee that you'll pay for them when you get to New York?"

"No, I'll pay for them in cash."

"Then what's the favor?"

"To establish our *bona fides.* To approve our being listed under different names than those on our passports."

136

"Just that?"

"Yes."

"But my dear sir"—Courtney was relieved and amused —"that's nothing. Thousands of people travel incognito. You don't need the sanction of the embassy for that!"

"That may be. But," Wolfe persisted, "I thought it desirable to take this precaution. With all the restrictions imposed nowadays on people who wish to move around, or need to, I wanted to preclude any possibility of a snag. Also I prefer not to undertake lengthy explanations to a clerk in a steamship office. Will you phone them?"

Courtney smiled. "This is a pleasant surprise, Mr. Wolfe. Certainly I'll phone them. I wish all the favors our fellow citizens ask for were as simple. And now I hope you won't mind if I ask for a favor from you. After I told Mr. Teague, the Secretary, that you were coming here this afternoon, he must have spoken of it to the Ambassador, because he told me later that the Ambassador would like to meet you. So if you can spare a few minutes, after I phone?"

Wolfe was frowning. "She's a woman."

"Yes, indeed."

"I must ask your forbearance. I'm tired clear to my bones, and I must catch a seven-o'clock plane to Genoa. Unless—will you take it ill and change your mind about phoning?"

"My God, no!" Courtney laughed. He drew his head back and roared. It struck me as pretty boisterous for a diplomat.

XVI

At noon the next day, Friday, we sat in our cabin on B deck on the *Basilia*. She was to sail at one. Everything was under control except one thing. At the Forelli Hotel in Genoa we had eleven hours sleep on good mattresses, and a good breakfast. Wolfe could walk without shuffling or staggering, and my bruises weren't quite as raw. We were listed as Carl Gunther and Alex Gunther, had paid for the tickets, and had a little over six hundred bucks in our jeans. It was an outside cabin, twice as big as our cell in the Bari can, with two beds and two chairs, and one of

137

the chairs was upholstered and Wolfe could squeeze into it.

But what about Peter Zov?

All Wolfe had been told was that he would enter Italy at Gorizia Wednesday night, cross to Genoa by way of Padua and Milan, and be on the *Basilia* as a cabin steward by Thursday night. Wolfe had wanted to know what his name would be, but Stritar had said that would be decided after he got to Genoa. Of course we knew nothing about where Zov would get his name or his papers, or from whom, or how the fix was set up for him to replace a steward. We didn't know how good the fix was, or whether it always worked or only sometimes. As we sat there in the cabin, we didn't give a damn about any of that; all that was eating us was, was he on board or not? If he wasn't, did we want to sail anyhow and hope he would come later? Didn't we have to? If we abandoned ship just because Zov didn't show up, wouldn't that be a giveaway?

"There's an hour left," I said. "I'll go and look around some more. Stewards are popping in and out everywhere."

"Confound it." Wolfe hit the chair arm with his fist. "We should have kept him with us."

"Stritar would have smelled a rat if you had insisted on it, and anyway he wouldn't buy it."

"Pfui. What is ingenuity for? I should have managed it. I'm a dunce. I should have foreseen this and prevented it. By heaven, I won't start back without him!"

There was a knock at the door, I said, "Come in," it opened, and Peter Zov entered with our bags.

"Oh, it's you," he said in Serbo-Croat. He put the bags down and turned to go.

"Wait a minute," Wolfe said. "There is something to say."

"You can say it later. This is a busy time."

"Just one word, then. Don't go to any pains to keep us from hearing you speak English. Of course you do—some, at least—or you couldn't be a cabin steward on this boat."

"You're smart," he said in Serbo-Croat. "Okay," he said in American, and went.

Wolfe told me to shut the door, and I did. When I turned back he had his eyes closed and was sighing, deep, and then again, deeper. He opened his eyes, looked at the bags and then at me, and told me what had been said.

"We ought to know his name," I suggested.

"We will. Go on deck and watch the gangway. He might take it into his head to skedaddle."

"Why should he?"

"He shouldn't. But a man with his frontal lobes pushed back like that is unpredictable. Go."

So I was on deck, at the rail, when we shoved off, and had a good look at the city stretching along the strip at the edge of the water and climbing the hills. The hills might have impressed me more if I hadn't just returned from a jaunt in Montenegro. By the time we had cleared the outer harbor and were in open water most of my fellow passengers had gone below for lunch, and I decided that now was as good a time as any for getting a certain point settled.

I went back down to the cabin and told Wolfe, "It's lunchtime. You've decided to stay put in this cabin all the way across, and you may be right. It's not likely that there's anyone on board who would recognize you, but it's possible, and if it happened and it got around, as it would, the best that could result would be that you'd have to write another script. But we're going to see a lot of each other in the next twelve days, not to mention the last six, and I think it would be bad policy for us to eat all our meals together in this nook."

"So do I."

"I'll eat in the dining room."

"By all means. I've already given Peter Zov my order for lunch."

"What?" I stared. "Zov?"

"Certainly. He's our steward."

"Good God. He'll bring all your meals and you'll eat them?"

"Yes. It will be trying, and it won't help my digestion, but it will have its advantages. I'll have plenty of opportunities to discuss our plans."

"And if he gets ideas and mixes in some arsenic?"

"Nonsense. Why should he?"

"He shouldn't. But a man with his frontal lobes pushed back like that is unpredictable."

"Go get your lunch."

I went, and found that though eating in the dining room would provide a change, it would offer nothing spectacular in companionship. Table Seventeen seated six. One chair was empty and would be all the way, and the other four were occupied by a German who thought he could speak English but was mistaken, a woman from Maryland who spoke it too much, and a mother and daughter, Italian or something, who didn't even know "dollar" and "okay" and

139

"cigarette." The daughter was seventeen, attractive, and almost certainly a smoldering volcano of Latin passion, but even if I had been in the humor to try stirring up a young volcano, which I wasn't, mamma stayed glued to her all the way over.

During the twelve days there was plenty of time, of course, to mosey around and make acquaintances and chin at random, but by the third day I had learned that the only three likely prospects, not counting the volcano, were out. One, a black-eyed damsel with a lisp, was on her way to Pittsburgh to get married. Another, a tall slender Nordic who needed no makeup and used none, loved to play chess, and that was all. The third, a neat little blonde, started drinking Gibsons an hour before lunch and didn't stop. One morning I decided to do some research in physiology and keep up with her, but late in the afternoon I saw that she was cheating. There were two of her, and they could both float around in the air. So I called it off, fought my way down to the cabin, and flopped on the bed. Wolfe shot me a glance but had no comment. In Genoa he had bought a few dozen books, all in Italian, and apparently had bet himself he would clean them up by the time we sighted Sandy Hook.

He and I did converse now and then during the voyage, but not too cordially, because of a basic difference of opinion. I completely disapproved of the plan which he wanted opportunity to discuss with Peter Zov. The argument had started in the hotel at Genoa and had continued, off and on, ever since. My first position had been that the way to handle it was to wait until we were well at sea, the second or third day, and then see the captain and tell him Zov had committed a murder in New York and had the weapon with him, and ask him to lock Zov up, and find his gun and take it, and radio Inspector Cramer of the New York Police Department to meet the boat at Quarantine. Wolfe had rejected it on the ground that the New York police had never heard of Zov and would probably radio the captain to that effect, and with nothing but our word, unsupported by evidence, the captain would refuse to act; and not only that, but also the captain, or someone he told about it, might warn Zov and even arrange somehow to get him off the ship before we reached American waters. On the high seas there was no jurisdiction but the captain's. If not the captain himself, someone on board with some authority must be a Communist, or at least a friend of the Tito regime, or how could it be arranged to get Zov on as a steward whenever they wanted to?

So I took a new position. As soon as we entered the North River everyone on board, including the captain, would be under the jurisdiction of the New York police, and Wolfe could call Cramer on the ship-to-shore phone, give him the picture, and tell him to meet the boat at the pier. That way there couldn't possibly be any slip. Even if the whole damn crew and half the officers were Commies, there was nothing they could do if Sergeant Stebbins once got his paws on Zov and the Luger.

Wolfe didn't try to talk me out of that one; he just vetoed it, and that was the argument. It wasn't only that he was pigheaded. It was his bloated conceit. He wanted to sit in his own chair at his desk in his office, with a bottle of beer and a glass in front of him, tell me to get Cramer on the phone, pick up his instrument, and say in a casual tone, "Mr. Cramer? I've just got home from a little trip. I have the murderer of Marko Vukcic here, and the weapon, and I can tell you where to get witnesses to testify that he was in New York on March eighteenth. Will you please send someone to get him? Oh, you'll come yourself? At your convenience. Mr. Goodwin, who was with me on the trip, has him safely in charge."

That was his plan. The *Basilia* was scheduled to dock at noon on Wednesday. We would disembark and go home. That evening after dark Zov would come ashore and meet me at a waterfront bar, to go with me to the house of a friend of ours who would lend us his car to drive to Philadelphia. The house would be on West Thirty-fifth Street. I would take Zov in and introduce him to Nero Wolfe, taking adequate precautions that he didn't execute his mission then and there. Possibly Wolfe would have to get Cramer on the phone himself instead of telling me to.

Wolfe wouldn't budge. That was the plan, no matter what I said, or how often I said it, about the risks involved or the defects in Wolfe's character that made him hatch it. I admit that my remarks about the defects got fairly pointed by the twelfth day, and that morning as we packed, him with his bag on his bed and me with mine on mine, our relations were so strained that when he had prolonged trouble with his zipper he didn't call for help and I didn't offer any. When I had my bag closed and labeled I told him, "See you in the dining room with the immigration officers," and left him. Out in the passage there was Zov, coming along. He asked, "Okay?" and I told him, "Yep, okay." He entered our cabin. Being good and sore, I told my legs to go on to the dining room, but they said no. They kept me standing there until Zov came out again with our bags, and headed for the stairs. I wanted to stop him and make sure he knew where we were going to meet that evening, but Wolfe had said it was all arranged in Serbo-Croat, and the few times I had tried exchanging English with Zov it hadn't worked too well, so I skipped it.

When we had finished immigrating, Wolfe went back to the cabin and I went on deck to take in the harbor and the Statue of Liberty and the skyline. The neat little blonde came and joined me at the rail, and if you had guessed her Gibson intake from the way she looked you would have been away off. She was just a happy and healthy little doll with nice clear eyes and a clear, smooth skin, so much so that a news photographer, who had taken a dozen shots of the only notable on board, an orchestra conductor, and was looking around for something that might appeal to his public, came and asked her to pose. She said all right, but refused to sit on the rail with her skirt up, and I thought it might have been worth the trouble to try to reform her. There was nothing wrong with her legs, so it wasn't that.

It was a bright, sunny day. As we passed the Battery and slid up the river I was thinking that now would be the time to telephone Cramer if that big baboon had listened to reason. It would be a crime if something happened now to spoil it—as, for instance, Zov deciding he liked some other contact in New York better than us. I had a notion to go down to the cabin and have one more try at talking sense into Wolfe, and was debating it as we were being nosed into the slip, when his voice sounded behind me and I turned. He was looking placid and pleased. He glanced left and right at the line of waving passengers and then down at the group of waving welcomers on the pier. He nodded at somebody, and I stretched my neck to see who it was, and there was Zov with three or four other stewards, back against the bulkhead.

"Satisfactory," Wolfe said.

"Yeah," I agreed. "So far."

Somebody yelled, "Nero Wolfe!"

I jerked around. It was the news photographer. He was headed for us down the deck, beaming, jostling passengers. "Mr. Wolfe! Look this way! Just a second!" He advanced and got set to focus.

It may have been partly me. If I hadn't looked at Zov and started my hand inside my jacket he might have hesitated long enough for Wolfe to get behind something or somebody. He was fast. I never saw a faster hand. Mine had just touched the butt of the Marley when he pulled the trigger. Wolfe took one step toward him and went down. I had the Marley out but couldn't shoot because the other stewards were all over Zov. I jumped over Wolfe's body and was there to help, but they had Zov flat on the deck, and one of them had his gun. I went back to Wolfe, who was on his side, propping himself with an elbow. People were crowding in and jabbering.

"Lie down," I commanded him. "Where did he get you?"

"Leg. Left leg."

I squatted and looked. The hole was in the left leg of his pants, ten inches above the knee. I wanted to laugh, and I don't know why I didn't. Maybe I was afraid the photographer would shoot it and it would look silly.

"Probably in the bone," I said. "What did I tell you?"

"Have they got him?"

"Yes."

"The gun?"

"Yes."

"Was it the Luger?"

"Yes."

"Satisfactory. Find a phone and get Mr. Cramer."

He flattened out and closed his eyes. The ham.

ABOUT THE AUTHOR

REX STOUT, the creator of Nero Wolfe, was born in Noblesville, Indiana, in 1886, the sixth of nine children of John and Lucetta Todhunter Stout, both Quakers. Shortly after his birth, the family moved to Wakarusa, Kansas. He was educated in a country school, but, by the age of nine, was recognized throughout the state as a prodigy in arithmetic. Mr. Stout briefly attended the University of Kansas, but left to enlist in the Navy, and spent the next two years as a warrant officer on board President Roosevelt's yacht. When he left the Navy in 1908, Rex Stout began to write freelance articles, worked as a sightseeing guide and as an itinerant bookkeeper. Later he devised and implemented a school banking system which was installed in four hundred cities and towns throughout the country. In 1927 Mr. Stout retired from the world of finance and, with the proceeds of his banking scheme, left for Paris to write serious fiction. He wrote three novels that received favorable reviews before turning to detective fiction. His first Nero Wolfe novel, *Fer-de-Lance*, appeared in 1934. It was followed by many others, among them, *Too Many Cooks, The Silent Speaker, If Death Ever Slept, The Doorbell Rang* and *Please Pass the Guilt*, establishing Nero Wolfe as a leading character on a par with Erle Stanley Gardner's famous protagonist, Perry Mason. During the war, Rex Stout waged a personal campaign against Nazism as chairman of the War Writers' Board, master of ceremonies of the radio program "Speaking of Liberty" and as a member of several national committees. After the war, he turned his attention to mobilizing public opinion against the wartime use of thermonuclear devices, was an active leader in the Authors' Guild and resumed writing his Nero Wolfe novels. All together, his Nero Wolfe novels have been translated into twenty-two languages and have sold more than forty-five million copies. Rex Stout died in 1975 at the age of eighty-eight. A month before his death, he published his forty-sixth Nero Wolfe novel, *A Family Affair*.

• *A NERO WOLFE MYSTERY* •

Here are special advance preview chapters from THE BLOODIED IVY, the new Nero Wolfe novel by Robert Goldsborough, a Bantam hardcover now available at your local bookseller.

THE
BLOODIED IVY

Robert Goldsborough

NERO WOLFE RETURNS
IN A BANTAM DOUBLE AUDIO
CASSETTE ABRIDGEMENT
OF THE BLOODIED IVY!

ONE

Hale Markham's death had been big news, of Ocourse. It was even the subject of a brief conversation I had with Nero Wolfe. We were sitting in the office, he with beer and I with a Scotch-and-water, going through our copies of the *Gazette* before dinner.

"See where this guy up at Prescrott U. fell into a ravine on the campus and got himself killed?" I asked, to be chatty. Wolfe only grunted, but I've never been one to let a low-grade grunt stop me. "Wasn't he the one whose book—they mention it here in the story: *Bleeding Hearts Can Kill*—got you so worked up a couple of years back?"

Wolfe lowered his paper, sighed, and glared at a spot on the wall six inches above my head. "The man was a political Neanderthal," he rumbled. "He would have been supremely happy in the court of Louis XIV. And the book to which you refer is a monumental exercise in fatuity." I sensed the subject was closed, so I grunted myself and turned to the sports pages.

I probably wouldn't have thought any more about that scrap of dialogue except now, three weeks later, a small, balding, fiftyish specimen with brown-rimmed glasses and a sportcoat that could have won a blue ribbon in a quilting contest perched on the red leather chair in the office and stubbornly repeated the statement that had persuaded me to see him in the first place.

"Hale Markham was murdered," he said. "I'm unswerving in this conviction."

Let me back up a bit. The man before me had a name: Walter Willis Cortland. He had called the day before, Monday, introducing himself as a political science professor at Prescott University and a colleague of the late Hale Markham's. He then dropped the bombshell that Markham's death had not been a mishap.

I had asked Cortland over the phone if he'd passed his contention along to the local cops. "It's no contention, Mr. Goodwin, it's a fact," he'd snapped, adding that he had indeed visited the town police in Prescott, but they hadn't seemed much interested in what he had to say. I could see why: Based on what little he told me over the phone, Cortland didn't have a scrap of evidence to prove Markham's tumble was murder, nor did he seem inclined, in his zeal for truth, to nominate a culprit. So why, you ask, had I agreed to see him? Good question. I must admit it was at least partly vanity.

When he phoned at ten-twenty that morning and I answered "Nero Wolfe's office, Archie Goodwin speaking," Cortland had cleared his throat twice, paused, and said, "Ah, yes, Mr. Archie Goodwin. You're really the one with whom I wish to converse.

I've read about your employer, Nero Wolfe, and how he devotes four hours every day, nine to eleven before lunch and four to six in the afternoon, to the sumptuous blooms on the roof of your brownstone. That's why I chose this time to call. I also know how difficult it is to galvanize Mr. Wolfe to undertake a case, but that you have a reputation for being a bit more, er . . . open-minded.''

"If you're saying I'm easy, forget it," I said. "Somebody has to screen Mr. Wolfe's calls, or who knows what he'd be having to turn down himself—requests to find missing wives, missing parakeets, and even missing gerbils. And believe me when I tell you that Mr. Wolfe hates gerbils.''

Cortland let loose with a tinny chuckle that probably was supposed to show he appreciated my wry brand of humor, then cleared his throat, which probably was supposed to show that now he was all business. "Oh, no, no, I didn't mean that you were . . . uh, to use your term, easy,'' he stumbled, trying valiantly to recover.

"No, I, uh . . .'' He seemed to lose his way and cleared his throat several times before his mental processes kicked in again. "It's just that from what I've heard and read, anybody who has any, uh, hope of enticing Nero Wolfe to undertake a case has to approach you first. And that I am most willing to do. Most willing, Mr., er . . . Goodwin. I braced for another throat-clearing interlude, and sure enough, it arrived on schedule. If this was his average conversational speed, the phone company must love the guy.

"It's just that from what I've heard and read, anybody who has any hope of enticing Nero Wolfe to take a case has to approach you first. And that I am most willing to do. Most willing, Mr. Goodwin.''

He treated me once again to the sound of him clearing his throat. ''I will lay my jeremiad before you and you alone, and trust you to relay it accurately to Mr. Wolfe. You have a reputation, if I am not mistaken, for reporting verbatim conversations of considerable duration.''

Okay, so he was working on me. I knew it—after all, he had the sublety of a jackhammer, but maybe that was part of his charm, if you could use that term on such a guy. And I was curious as to just what ''information'' he had about the late Hale Markham's death. Also, the word ''jeremiad'' always gets my attention.

''All right,'' I told him, ''I'll see you tomorrow. What about ten in the morning?'' He said that was fine, and I gave him the address of Wolfe's brownstone on West Thirty-fifth Street near the Hudson.

The next day he rang our doorbell at precisely ten by my watch, which was one point in his favor. I've already described his appearance, which didn't surprise me at all when I saw him through the one-way glass in our front door. His looks matched his phone voice, which at least gave him another point for consistency. I let him in, shook a small but moderately firm paw, and ushered him to the red leather chair at the end of Wolfe's desk. So now you're up to speed, and we can go on.

''Okay, Mr. Cortland,'' I said, seated at my desk and turning to face him, ''you've told me twice, on the phone and just now, that your colleague Hale Markham did not accidentally stumble down that ravine. Tell me more.'' I flipped open my notebook and poised a pen.

Cortland gave a tug at the knot of his blue wool tie and nudged his glasses up on his nose by pushing on one lens with his thumb, which probably explained why the glass was so smeared. "Yes. Well, perhaps I should discourse in commencement about Hale, although I'm sure you know something of him."

When I'd translated that, I nodded. "A little. I know, for instance, that he was a political conservative, to put it mildly, that he once had a newspaper column that ran all over the country, that he had written some books, and that he was more than a tad controversial."

"Succinct though superficial," Cortland said, sounding like a teacher grading his pupil. He studied the ceiling as if seeking divine guidance in choosing his next words—or else trying to reboard his train of thought. "Mr. Goodwin, Hale Markham was one of the few, uh, truly profound political thinkers in contemporary America. And like so many of the brilliant and visioned, he was constantly besieged and challenged, not just from the left, but from specious conservatives as well." He paused for breath, giving me the opportunity to cut in, but because it looked like he was on a roll I let him keep going, lest he lose his way.

"Hale was uncompromising in his philosophy, Mr. Goodwin, which is one of the myriad reasons I admired him and was a follower—a disciple, if you will. And do not discount this as mere idle palaver—I think I'm singularly qualified to speak—after all, I had known him nearly half again a score of years. Hale took a position and didn't back away. He was fiercely combative and outspoken in his convictions."

"Which were?" I asked after figuring out that half again a score is thirty.

Cortland spread his hands, palms up. "How to begin?" he said, rolling his eyes. "Among other things, that the federal government, with its welfare programs and its intrusions into other areas of the society where it has no business, has steadily—if sometimes unwittingly—been attenuating the moral fiber of the nation, and that government's size and scope must be curtailed. He had a detailed plan to reduce the government in stages over a twenty-year period. Its fundamental caveat was—"

"I get the general idea. He must have felt pretty good about Reagan."

"Oh, up to a point." Cortland fiddled some more with his tie and pushed up his glasses again with a thumb, blinking twice. "But he believed, and I concur, that the President has never truly been committed to substantially reducing the federal government's scope. The man is far more form than substance."

That was enough political philosophy to hold me. "Let's get to Markham's death," I suggested. "You say you're positive his fall down that ravine was no accident. Why?"

Cortland folded his arms and looked at the ceiling again. "Mr. Goodwin, for one thing, Hale walked a great deal." He took a deep breath as if trying to think what to say next, and he was quiet for so long that I had to stare hard at him to get his engine started again. "In recent years, walking had been his major form of exercise. Claimed it expurgated his mind. Almost every night, he followed the identical course, which he informed me was almost exactly four miles. He started from his house, just off campus, and the route took him past the Student Union and the Central Quadrangle, then around the library and through an area called the Old Oaks and then—have you ever been up to Prescott, Mr. Goodwin?''

''Once, years ago, for a football game, against Rutgers. Your boys kicked a field goal to win, right at the end. It was quite an upset.''

Cortland allowed himself a sliver-thin smile, which was apparently the only kind he had, then nodded absently. ''Yes . . . now that you mention it, I think I remember. Probably the only time we ever beat them. We had a . . . Rhodes Scholar in the backfield. Extraordinary chap. Name escapes me. Lives in Sri Lanka now, can't recall why.'' He shook his head and blinked. ''Where was I? Oh, yes. Anyway, you should recall how hilly the terrain for our campus is, which isn't surprising, given that we're so close to the Hudson. Innumerable times, Prescott has been cited as the most picturesque university in the nation. There are several ravines cutting through it, and the biggest one is named Caldwell's Gash—I believe after one of the first settlers to the area. It's maybe one hundred fifty feet deep, with fairly steep sides, and the Old Oaks, a grove of trees that looks to me like it's getting perilously decrepit, is along one side of the Gash. Hale's walk always took him through the Oaks and fairly close to the edge of the Gash.''

''Is there a fence?''

''A fence?'' Another long pause as Cortland reexamined the ceiling, ''Yes, yes, there had been—there was . . . years ago. But at some point, it must have fallen apart, and never got replaced. The paved, uh, bicycle path through the Oaks is quite a distance from the edge—maybe thirty feet—and there are warning signs posted. On his postprandial strolls, though, Hale sometimes left the path—I know, I've walked with him many a time—and took a course somewhat closer to the edge.''

"So who's to say your friend didn't get a little too close just this once and go over the cliff?''

"Not Hale Markham,'' Cortland shook his small head vigorously, sending his glasses halfway down his nose. "This was a dedicated walker. He even wore hiking boots, for instance. And he was very surefooted—his age, which happened to be seventy-three, shouldn't deceive you. During his younger days, he'd done quite a bit of serious mountain climbing, both out west and, er, in the Alps. No, sir, Hale would not under any circumstances have slipped over the edge of the Gash.''

"Was the ground wet or muddy at the time?''

"It had not rained for days.''

"What about suicide?''

He bristled. "Unconceivable! Hale reveled in life too much. His health was good, remarkably good for his age. No note of any kind was discovered. I should know—I checked through his papers at home. I'm the executor of his estate.''

"What about an autopsy?''

"No autopsy. The doctor who examined the body said Hale died of a broken neck, a tragic consequence of the fall. He estimated the time of death to have been between ten and midnight. And the medical examiner set it down as accidental death. But there really wasn't any kind of an investigation to speak of. Most distressing.''

"All right,'' I said, "let's assume for purposes of

discussion that there is a murderer. Care to nominate any candidates?''

Cortland squirmed in the red leather chair, and twice he started to say something, but checked himself. He looked like he was having gas pains.

I gave him what I think of as my earnest smile. ''Look, even though you're not a client—not yet, anyway—I'm treating this conversation as confidential. Now, if you have *evidence* of a murder—that's different. Then, as a law-abiding, God-fearing, licensed private investigator, I'd have to report it to the police. But my guess is you don't have evidence. Am I right?''

He nodded, but still looked like something he ate didn't sit well with him. Then he did more squirming. The guy was getting on my nerves.

''Mr. Cortland, I appreciate your not wanting to come right out and call someone a murderer without evidence, but if I can get Mr. Wolfe to see you—and I won't guarantee it—he's going to press pretty hard. You can hold out on me, but he'll demand at the very least some suppositions. Do you have any?''

Cortland made a few more twitchy movements, crossed his legs, and got more fingerprints on his lenses. ''There were a number of people at Prescott who . . . weren't exactly fond of Hale,'' he said, avoiding my eyes. ''I'd, uh, chalk a lot of it up to jealousy.''

''Let's get specific. But first, was Markham married?''

''He had been, but his wife died, almost ten years ago.''

''Any children?''

''None. He was devoted to Lois—that was his wife. She was one of a kind, Mr. Goodwin. I'm a bachelor, always have been, but if I'd ever been fortunate enough to meet a woman like Lois Markham, my life would have taken a Byronic richness that . . . no matter, it's in the past. As far as children are concerned, Hale told me once that it was a major disappointment to both him and Lois that they never had a family.''

''What about relatives?''

''He had one brother, who had been deceased for years. His only living relative is a niece, unmarried, in California. He left her about fifty thousand dollars, plus his house. I've been trying to get her to venture here to go through Hale's effects—we can't begin to contemplate selling the place until it is cleaned out, which will be an extensive chore. Hale lived there for more than thirty years.''

''Has the niece said anything about when she might come east?''

''I've talked to her on the phone several times, and she keeps procrastinating,'' Cortland whined. ''When I spoke to her last week, she promised that she'd arrive here before Thanksgiving. We'll see.''

''Okay, you mentioned jealousy earlier. Who envied Markham?''

He lifted his shoulders and let them drop. ''Oh, any number of people. For one, Keith Potter.'' He eyed me as if expecting a reaction.

''Well, of course,'' I said. ''Why didn't I think of him myself? Okay—I give up. Who's Keith Potter?''

Cortland looked at me as if I'd just jumped out of a spaceship nude. ''Keith Potter is none other than the beloved president of Prescott.'' He touched his forehead with a flourish that was probably supposed to be a dazzling gesture of sarcasm.

"Why was Potter jealous of Markham?"

I got another one of those long-suffering-teacher-working-with-a-dense-student looks. "Partly because Hale was better known than Potter. In fact, Hale was arguably the most celebrated person in the university's history. And we've had *three* Nobel prize laureates through the years."

I nodded to show I was impressed. "So the president of the school resented its superstar teacher. Is that so unusual? I don't know much about the academic world, but one place or another I've gathered the impression that most colleges have a teacher or two who are often better known than the people who run the place."

"Unusual? I suppose not. But Potter—excuse me, *Doctor* Potter—is an empire builder. His not-so-secret goal is to sanctify his name by increasing the endowment to Prescott, thereby allowing him to erect more new buildings on the campus. The edifice complex, you know?" Cortland chuckled, crossed his arms over his stomach, and simpered.

"I don't mean to sound like a broken record, but that's not so unusual either, is it? Or such a bad thing for the university?"

"Maybe not," Cortland conceded, twitching. "If it's accompanied by a genuine respect for scholarship and research, uh, things that all schools aspiring to greatness should stress. But Potter desires, in effect, to upraise a monument to himself. That goal easily eclipses any desire on his part to improve the facilities purely for academic reasons."

I was itching to ask if the ends didn't justify the means, but Wolfe would be coming down from the plant rooms soon, so I pushed on. "How did Potter's obsession with buildings affect his relationship with Markham?''

Cortland sniffed. "Ah, yes, I was about to get to that, wasn't I? Potter had fastened onto Leander Bach and was working to get a bequest out of him—a considerable one. I assume you know who Bach is?'' I could tell by his tone that I'd shaken his faith in my grasp of current events.

"The eccentric multimillionaire?''

"That's one way of describing the man. I prefer to think of him as left-leaning to the point of irrationality. And that was the rub: The talk all over campus was that Bach wouldn't give a cent of his millions to the school as long as Hale was on the faculty. He had the gall to call Hale a Neanderthal.''

I stifled a smile, then shot a glance at my watch, "Mr. Wolfe will be down soon,'' I said. "And I—''

"Yes, I've been monitoring the time, as well,'' Cortland cut in. "And we've still got six minutes. Mr. Goodwin, as you can appreciate, my stipend as a university professor hardly qualifies me as a plutocrat. However, I've had the good fortune to inherit a substantial amount from my family. Because of that, I can comfortably afford Mr. Wolfe's fees, which I'm well aware are thought by some to border on extortionate. And I can assure you that this check,'' he said, reaching into the breast pocket of his crazy-quilt sportcoat, "has the pecuniary financial condition, feel free to call Cyrus Griffin, president of the First Citizens Bank of Prescott. I'll supply you with the number.''

"Not necessary,'' I said, holding up a hand and studying the check, drawn on Mr. Griffin's bank and made out to Nero Wolfe in the amount of twenty-five thousand dollars.

"That's just a good-faith retainer," Cortland said. "To show Mr. Wolfe—and you—that I'm earnest. I will be happy to match that amount on the completion of Mr. Wolfe's investigation, regardless, of its eventuation."

I tapped the check with a finger. Our bank balance could use this kind of nourishment—we hadn't pulled in a big fee in almost three months, and I was beginning to worry, even if the big panjandrum wasn't. But then, he almost never deigned to look at the checkbook. Such concerns were beneath him. Even if Wolfe refused to take Cortland on as a client, though, it would be instructive to see his reaction to somebody else who tosses around four-syllable, ten-dollar words like he does.

Maybe I could talk somebody into making a syndicated TV show out of their conversations and call it "The Battle of the Dictionary Dinosaurs." All right, so I was getting carried away, but what the hell, it *would* be fun to see these guys go at it. Besides, I'd pay admission to watch Wolfe's reaction to Cortland's mid-sentence ramblings.

"Okay, I'll hang onto this for now," I said to the little professor. "It may help me get Mr. Wolfe to see you, but I can't guarantee anything. I'll have to ask you to wait in the front room while we talk. If things go badly—and I always refuse to predict how he'll react—you may not get to see him, at least not today. But I'll try."

"I'm more than willing to remain here and plead my case with him directly." Cortland squared his narrow shoulders.

"Trust me. This is the best way to handle the situation. Now let's get you settled." I opened the soundproofed door and escorted the professor into the front room, then went down the hall to the kitchen to let Fritz know we had a guest so that he would monitor the situation. It simply wouldn't do to have people wandering through the brownstone.

That done, I returned to the office, where I just had time to get settled at my desk when the rumble of the elevator told me Wolfe was on his way down from the roof.

NERO WOLFE STEPS OUT

Every Wolfe Watcher knows that the world's largest detective wouldn't dream of leaving the brownstone on 35th street, with Fritz's three star meals, his beloved orchids and the only chair that actually suits him. But when an ultra-conservative college professor winds up dead and Archie winds up in jail, Wolfe is forced to brave the wilds of upstate New York to find a murderer.

THE BLOODIED IVY

by Robert Goldsborough

☐ 27816 $3.95

and don't miss these other Nero Wolfe mysteries by Robert Goldsborough:

☐	27024	**DEATH ON DEADLINE**	$3.95
☐	27938	**MURDER IN E MINOR**	$3.95
		"A Smashing Success"	
		—*Chicago Sun-Times*	
☐	05383	**THE LAST COINCIDENCE**	$16.95

And Bantam still offers you a whole series of Nero Wolfe mysteries by his creator, Rex Stout

☐	27819	**FER-DE-LANCE**	$3.50
☐	27828	**DEATH TIMES THREE**	$3.95
☐	27291	**THE BLACK MOUNTAIN**	$3.50
☐	27776	**IN THE BEST FAMILIES**	$3.50
☐	27290	**TOO MANY COOKS**	$3.50
☐	27780	**THE GOLDEN SPIDERS**	$3.50
☐	25363	**PLOT IT YOURSELF**	$3.50
☐	24813	**THREE FOR THE CHAIR**	$3.50

Look for them at your bookstore or use this page to order:

Kinsey Millhone is...

"The best new private eye."   *—The Detroit News*

"A tough-cookie with a soft center."   *—Newsweek*

"A stand-out specimen of the new female operatives."
—Philadelphia Inquirer

Sue Grafton is...

The Shamus and Anthony Award winning creator of Kinsey Millhone and quite simply one of the hottest new mystery writers around.

Bantam is...

The proud publisher of Sue Grafton's Kinsey Millhone mysteries:

Special Offer
Buy a Bantam Book
for only 50¢.

Now you can have Bantam's catalog filled with hundreds of titles plus take advantage of our unique and exciting bonus book offer. A special offer which gives you the opportunity to purchase a Bantam book for only 50¢. Here's how!

By ordering any five books at the regular price per order, you can also choose any other single book listed (up to a $5.95 value) for just 50¢. Some restrictions do apply, but for further details why not send for Bantam's catalog of titles today!

Just send us your name and address and we will send you a catalog!